Roddy Murray

George Milne Must Die

© Roddy Murray 2017

Roddy Murray asserts the moral right to be identified as the author of this work.

Acknowledgments

I would like to thank everyone who has encouraged me to complete this book. In particular I would like to thank my brother Sandy and Margaret Rustad for patiently correcting and sub-editing the manuscript.

By the same author:

George Milne – Cat Detective

George Milne – Murder at the Butler's Convention

The Treasure Hunters

A Snow White Scenario

Body and Soul

For my parents and for my children.

Chapter One - Janine's Return

Ever since Janine had discovered that George had been, albeit reluctantly, having an affair with Lola Cortez and confronted them both during rehearsals for Lola's knife throwing act in Edinburgh, George had lived alone. That was not strictly true, as he shared custody of Evelyn Cook with Janine's daughter Rosie and her partner Carol, but that didn't count. Although a still attractive woman in her 30s, Evelyn needed the security of others, due *both to* her learning difficulties and *to* her traumatic early life. George had always seen Evelyn and Frankie's suitcase of money as a joint undertaking and had ensured that Evelyn was looked after and had whatever she needed.

No, George had lived alone in the romantic sense: alone to the point of being able to get up when he wished, watch what he wanted to watch on TV and eat as many chocolate digestive biscuits as he wanted, along with his cups of tea or coffee; alone in the sense of not being constantly interrupted by conversations started from distant rooms regarding shopping, dress sizes or a mother's latest minor ailment; alone in the sense of living in peace and quiet. As a general state of affairs this was quite welcome from George's point of view. After all, he had been married to Glenda long enough to have longed for solitude at almost any cost.

He knew that this was unlikely to last. Experience had taught him that his life had a strange way of changing, even if he took no action himself. Slowly he became aware of Janine's reappearance in his domestic existence. It started with her covering occasional shifts at The Ranch during which they had had to converse. The conversations were initially short.

"A pint of special please" followed by "that'll be £2.80, there's your change".

But it was a start. It led to polite questions as to each other's health and so on from there.

On one occasion Janine asked if she could finally collect a bag of her things which had been left at George's house, and he sensed danger. He agreed, but when she mentioned a *time suitable* for her*self* he was pleased to note that he had a dentist's appointment and would not be present himself. A secret hiding place for a key was agreed in what was the longest conversation they had had for six months and the bag was duly collected. When George came home he noticed a picture or two had been straightened and a cloth run round the worst of the staining in his bathroom. His sense of foreboding grew.

The following day when he visited The Ranch, Janine thanked him for the bag of clothes and then, to his concern, steered the conversation round to the occasion when she had discovered George and Lola were sharing a room and a bed in The Pacific Grand Hotel in Edinburgh. George braced himself for an angry exchange but was even more worried when Janine adopted a conciliatory tone and even hinted that Lola may have taken advantage of his kind heart and relative innocence.

"Oh dear," thought George. "She wants to move back in."

Over the next few days George found a friendlier atmosphere in The Ranch during Janine's shifts and found the two of them talking and laughing on one or more occasions. He was not altogether upset by this turn of events and began to look forward to their conversations. Life was almost back to the happy days of flirting with the attractive barmaid in your local pub before returning to the peace and quiet of your own front room to watch the news before heading off to bed - a period of time in his life which he remembered fondly as containing the best of both worlds.

However, the notion that Janine had a different idea of their future relationship began to take hold in George's mind: the little things like Janine's references to past shared moments together; a forgiving joking reference to "that Spanish Slut" or the occasional pint on the house. Bigger things too added to the impression; mention of Janine having to move out of her rented flat, an uncertainty as to where she would live after that. Perhaps the biggest clue that Janine wanted to move back in came when she showed up on his doorstep one afternoon with three suitcases, willing to give their relationship one more chance.

George realised thereafter that he must have agreed, and after a long embrace during which Janine promised to let bygones be bygones they returned to a replica of their previous domestic arrangements. For George this meant a cleaner, fresher smelling house, female company every day, better meals but fewer visits to The Ranch. On balance he was happy to let events follow their inevitable course. Janine, for her part, seemed delighted to be back "home" as she quickly reverted to calling George's flat.

To cement the new arrangement Janine suggested they took a holiday together. Knowing George's preference for staying close to the familiar, she concentrated their options on short breaks within Scotland. Eventually they agreed to stay at a borrowed caravan belonging to Janine's cousin which was parked permanently during the summer in a large holiday complex called Mulligan's on the west coast. The resort had several hundred static caravans and space for tourers, with facilities to amuse all generations whatever the weather. It had everything from a series of swimming pools with water slides to a boating pond with pedalos. Janine read out the list to George from the website. Pony trekking, sauna, gym and sports complex were unlikely to see him pay them a visit but he warmed more to the idea of the three bars, the slot machines and the choice of restaurants. Janine was keen on the pony trekking, with or without him and they both might enjoy a dip in one of the pools. Dates were agreed and the caravan booked for a full week.

George even found himself rather looking forward to the adventure. After all, it was only a little bit of an adventure. There was no possibility of any real excitement or danger.

Chapter Two - An Inspector gets a Call

Janice Young had done well out of her experience assisting Jimmy Bell in Edinburgh - not from learning his secrets as a great detective. In that respect she had been rather disappointed. Prior to being posted as his second in command she had been as convinced as everyone else that he had put away some of Glasgow and Lanarkshire's hardest drug dealing criminals through his abilities as a detective. Instead she had found a man perhaps worried about living up to the reputation he had gained and on his own reluctant admission, a man who had been rather lucky in terms of the information which had fallen into his lap. Instrumental in his early success in the West of Scotland was the shady figure of one George Milne. Jimmy had been reticent about Milne's involvement when she had begun to work with him but had admitted, as their professional relationship developed, that without the SIM card Milne had passed to him at the funeral of drug king-pin Frankie Cook, it might have taken longer for him to corner as many crooks as he had. Janice later came to the conclusion that without that help from Milne, Jimmy would have got nowhere.

In their main case together, the murder of Billy Winkman by Lord Strathbole, Milne had again appeared as a person of interest. Her first impression of him had been of a hardened criminal masquerading in manner and costume as a clown, not so much from any evil demeanour, but rather from the fact that he always seemed to be about when people were brutally killed and she further concluded that nobody could be as innocent or stupid as Milne appeared to be. Jimmy had been adamant throughout that although evidence suggested Milne's involvement in the murders of both Winkman and Eric Ramsay, he was not a murderer. Janice had been convinced of the opposite but Jimmy had proved otherwise when again Milne produced a key piece of evidence to solve the case. Again she felt Jimmy would have got nowhere without Milne and as the blaze of publicity surrounding Strathbole's arrest and subsequent jailing for murder had boosted both their careers and led to her recent promotion to Detective Inspector she had almost forgotten the part George had played.

Since returning to the West Coast and being posted to Lanarkshire she had found herself occasionally with the time to re-assess her experience of working for Jimmy. Only occasionally though, as plenty of new faces had appeared from under rocks to fill the gaps left by Frankie Cook and the others who had been removed from circulation during Jimmy's time there. He had been very lucky with two big cases, it was true. The other cases she had worked on with him had shown him to be a plodding, average detective at best. Maybe his strength was knowing the right people to trust and who could provide information to him and persuading them to trust him. In this respect he had won a gold watch when George Milne had entered his life. She wouldn't trust Milne as far as she could throw him, which wouldn't have been far at all, keen white water swimmer as she was. He might appear all innocent and even cuddly in a strange, almost repulsive way but she sensed underneath all that was a hard man, capable of any crime and with the potential for extreme violence if necessary.

The details of Frankie Cook's death had never been fully established beyond the fact that Milne had been somewhere in the area at the time. How he had managed to escape further investigation on that account was a mystery to her. It seemed to be an error on Jimmy Bell's part but she certainly wasn't going to hint at such a failing in a newly promoted Detective Chief Inspector who had also ensured her recent promotion. That would be unwise in a career-minded Police Officer like herself. She would leave that for now, but if George Milne ever appeared in her sights again she would make sure that any unanswered questions were tidied up before she let him off the hook so easily.

"Oh yes," she thought, "he's a bad one right enough."

One day she was sitting in her office looking through mug-shots of local shop-lifters when her phone rang.

"Serg....Inspector Young," she answered, still not fully adjusted to her recent promotion.

"Hi Boss," said the voice at the other end of the line. "There's a patient escaped from Carstair's and he might be heading our way. Does the name Stevie 'Spider' Webb ring a bell?"

It vaguely did as a name from Jimmy Bell's stories but she couldn't put any details to it.

13

"Vaguely," she answered.

"He was one of Frankie Cook's enforcers and went down for various things including murder when George Milne and his missus helped collar him. Seems like he has never forgiven them and wants revenge. I remember the case from a few years back. Jimmy Bell put him away with others from Frankie's gang and a few of Glasgow's finest. I'll dig out the file and bring it down if you want."

"Yep, let's see what we've got," Janice replied. Her colleague, Detective Sergeant Bob 'Dixie' Dixon was a career police officer like herself and smart with it. He had a degree in forensic psychology and she hated him for it. Aside from that she liked working with him as he shared her businesslike approach to the job and rarely went for a pint after work like most of the other detectives she knew. This had the twin advantages of him always being able to legally drive and being available at a moment's notice to chase up leads when she needed it done.

Dixie appeared at her office door five minutes later with a thick file containing everything known about one Steven Webb, aka Spider Webb, currently aka most wanted criminal in the West of Scotland. Dixie had clearly read some of it before phoning his boss, not wanting to appear poorly informed if she needed any advice. She took the file and the coffee he had automatically brought for her and started to read the summary sheet. The automatic cups of coffee were another thing she liked about Dixie.

Spider was a bad man, she concluded very early on as she read his file. He had been convicted of the sadistic murder of one person and was implicated in the murder of at least two others, plus the abduction of Janine McGovern, girlfriend of one George Milne, with the intention of murder. There was that name again, she thought to herself. There was no way Milne was just an innocent bystander to half the crimes and criminals in the West of Scotland. He was in it up to his chubby little cheeks and at the first opportunity she was determined to prove it. Any excuse would do to search his house as a start. If that didn't turn up something she would eat her hat.

Dixie had logged into the spare computer in her office and was checking everything that he could about Spider's known haunts and criminal record. He had been in and out of prison as soon as he had been old enough to stop being in and out of juvenile detention. His early career was based in and around Liverpool with a suspected trip or two to London. Violence was part and parcel of his criminal activities, from assaulting one of his Primary School teachers onwards. His first serious prison term in Liverpool was for GBH at the age of 28. Prior to that witnesses seemed reluctant to appear in court to give evidence against him or had simply disappeared by the time of the trial. His mistake had been committing GBH on an off duty police officer who was more than happy to appear as a witness for the prosecution.

He had worked his way up to the role of enforcer for one of the drugs gangs on Merseyside and then, for no clear reason, moved to Lanarkshire. His reputation grew quickly there as an enforcer for Whacky Frank Cook. This arrangement had lasted several years and greatly assisted Frankie's rise to king pin in the industry there.

When Frankie had mysteriously fallen or been thrown off a third floor balcony in Coatshill, Spider had subsequently been arrested after escaping from custody in connection with a previously unsolved murder. Instead of making a run for it he had sought out Janine McGovern who had been instrumental in his arrest and forced her to drive towards what the police assumed would be a grisly death. Instead, aided by her partner George Milne, she had alerted a passing Police patrol who had recaptured Spider after a violent struggle.

Now he was on the loose again and, based on a diary found in his cell at the High Security State Hospital at Carstairs, he was hell-bent on finding both Janine and George Milne again. Dixie and Janice Young read this from different sets of notes at about the same time and quickly agreed they needed uniform branch to find Spider's targets and to guard them immediately. Thereafter a full search of all his known haunts in both Liverpool and Glasgow might turn up something.

After an hour or so it was clear that neither Milne nor Janine McGovern were at home or at the flat where Janine's daughter and her partner lived, and the search was widened. When Janice Young received the initial report that they could not be found at either address she did a double take.

"Dixie, where does McGovern's daughter live?" she asked.

Dixie looked at the computer in front of him.

"10 Woodend Walk," he replied. "Why?"

"Doesn't that ring a bell with you?"

"Fuck's sake," swore Dixie. "I can't believe I missed that. Frankie Cook dies in a mysterious fall at 10 Woodend Walk. His enforcer is arrested after help from George bloody Milne who was seen in the area at the time. George Milne lives with Janine McGovern, who just happens to beat Spider Webb to a pulp with her shoe, if you believe that one. Now with Frankie gone and Spider in Jail, McGovern's daughter moves into the flat which Frankie had used for his drug dealing empire. It says here that Frankie's sister, one Evelyn Cook, still lives there."

"Don't you see what that bastard Milne did?" said Janice in a fit of excitement. "Milne gets rid of the mob running Coatshill's drugs business and then takes over, putting his step daughter in to run it for him. He and McGovern must have been responsible for Frankie's death and the death of his sidekick Willie McBride. Frankie's sister Evelyn was either in on it or is being forced to help them. She must be the brains behind the day to day supply."

Dixie looked sceptical.

"There's a note from Jimmy Bell saying Evelyn has learning difficulties and was unable to provide any help when she was interviewed."

"Learning difficulties my arse," snapped Janice. "If Milne can convince people he is as stupid and as innocent as Jimmy believed him to be then this Evelyn can fake learning difficulties too."

"Milne must have connections all over the place," said Dixie. "Remember he mysteriously came up with the evidence to convict Lord what's-his-face."

"Strathbole," added Janice. "Bloody hell. Maybe Strathbole was into drugs and Milne needed him out of the way too. Dig out the files on the Strathbole case, everything you can on Frankie Cook, Steven Spider Webb, Willie McBride and anybody they have even had a pint with. We may or not find Spider in time to save Milne and his girlfriend but there is more to this than just an escape from custody. This is a battle over control of Lanarkshire's drugs trade and if I'm not mistaken, George Milne is now on the run from us and his nearest rival. Check with Merseyside too and see who Spider worked for. If they're behind his escape we could be in the middle of the biggest drugs war the UK has seen outside London."

"Christ," said Dixie unable to argue with his boss's assessment of the situation. If Milne was as dangerous as she thought and Spider was ordered to get rid of him by his Scouser bosses then there would be one hell of a battle when they met up, wherever it turned out to be.

Chapter Three - Hidden Treasure

When Janine moved back in with George he became rather anxious about the possibility of her finding the money which he had acquired from Frankie Cook: money which was still in the original suitcase but now resided in the darkest corner of the cupboard under the stairs rather than under the bed. He gave a great deal of thought to the best place to hide it and eventually decided that the garden shed made sense as Janine had absolutely no interest in gardening. Nor did he, he had to admit but he did escape to the shed from time to time for peace and quiet or to escape from some of Janine's friends or relatives when they visited. The tools in the shed were untroubled by frequent use but it contained a very comfortable seat and a wifi signal boosting box.

He waited till Janine was away to work one day and started digging inside the shed as quietly as he could. The shed had been built from a kit and rather than go to the inconvenience of constructing proper foundations, George had simply placed a concrete slab at each corner to support the weight. This left the main floor area largely as it had been before, or to be exact, lovely, fertile soil. He dug a hole large enough for the four polythene packages he had prepared earlier indoors and then put them inside with a spare fifth slab on top covered with compacted soil. When he had finished he was left with a fairly large pile of earth which he had to dispose of without anyone noticing what he was doing. Fortunately he had *watched* 'The Great Escape' every Christmas and knew just how to get rid of it.

In the upper flat of the four in a block, next door to George, lived retired bus driver Bob Brown. Bob had never liked George. They had come into conflict over boundaries, hedges and weeds or more accurately, Bob had shouted at George about these things over the years and George had shrugged his shoulders and walked away in a very provocative way, to Bob's way of thinking. Bob's way of thinking was different to most people's way of thinking though. He didn't like many people: children, pensioners, teenagers, young mothers with prams, smokers, non-smokers and everyone else. Anyone in fact who represented any group who had ever got on board any of the buses he had driven.

He had liked George's mother to the point of trying for more than just a New Year kiss shortly after she was widowed. Things had gone badly between the neighbours ever since and it was all George's fault as far as Bob was concerned. After all, it had been George who had shown him the door when his mother objected to Bob's advances. George had been told off by his mother for not being more aggressive on that occasion and literally just pointing at the door, but that was enough to upset Bob for life. He had a habit of watching George and Janine in particular on their rare visits to work in the garden and today was no exception. He had often watched George amble to the shed and had his own theories as to why he spent so much time there. He watched now as George appeared from the shed and walked slowly round the garden flower bed nearest the fence, scuffing the earth as he went.

"What is he up to now?" he wondered.

George returned to the shed only to reappear five minutes later with, Bob now noticed, bulging pockets. Again he walked around on the flower bed, dragging his feet as he went and the bulge in the pockets going down as he walked. This was repeated twenty times in total and Bob resolved to get a sample of the new material being spread as soon as it got dark. There was something suspicious about Milne at the best of times and this was clearly an attempt at damage to the area between the properties and *the* spread *of* death and destruction to the scrappy patch of mainly weeds on Bob's side. The earth in that area was the preferred toilet area of Bob's Staffordshire Pit Bull, Spike. The regular spraying of dog urine had rendered the soil incapable of growing anything attractive but Bob was convinced that George Milne was doing something to the soil out of spite.

Bob also believed that George had stolen some of the nicer weeds from that part of the garden as he had noticed better examples of all of them growing in earth on George's side of the fence. Stealing plants and poisoning soil. That was what Milne must have been up to for years. Until this moment he had never witnessed any such activity but now he felt he had proof positive. If he could prove there was any poison or weed killer in whatever was being furtively spread he would have Milne up in court. All he needed was proof. Milne was dodgy, very dodgy, and might even be guilty of illegally killing his neighbour's plants. If he was *guilty* he would feel the full weight of the law. Milne never seemed to tidy any of the common areas or help the retired couple below Bob with their bins. The fact that the couple had refused George's offers of help was of no consequence. Bob prided himself that nobody had ever travelled on one of his buses without a ticket and there was no way Milne was getting a free ride as one of his neighbours now.

George finished spreading the soil from inside his shed except for enough to cover the newly positioned slab which he had also covered with tools and old plant pots. He narrowly escaped serious injury when he stepped on his garden rake but by sheer luck managed to move his head aside as the handle sprung up and it hit his shoulder with little effect. He looked at the floor area of his shed and decided it looked innocent enough. He had some money with him for the next period of time and some more hidden in the boot of his car. The remainder of it should be safe enough now from Janine's attention and if she moved out again, which he never ruled out, he could bring it safely back indoors.

Chapter Four - The Holiday of a Lifetime

The day arrived for George and Janine to head off to the caravan park and he was pleasantly surprised to find that no disaster had befallen the preparations. The car was loaded the night before and even Evelyn had remained at home with Rosie and Carol. George was surprised to find himself looking forward to time away from the house, his favourite chair and relaxed cups of tea in front of the television. He found himself thinking more deeply than he liked to about the benefits of having a lady in his life. Perhaps his marriage to Glenda had coloured his outlook too much against co-habitation. It had certainly been an unpleasant and rather prolonged experience but he knew many men who were still with their wives and partners after far longer periods and seemed happy or at least contented with the arrangement. Willie Taylor was clearly still very much in love with his wife and, alone amongst George's acquaintances, never even joked about being unhappy nor was he ever critical of his wife. Perhaps, just perhaps, Janine was the one who could make the arrangement work for George.

The holiday in the caravan would prove the perfect testing ground for their long term relationship. If they could survive a week in the cramped caravan they could surely survive together in George's house.

For Janine's part, she was glad to be back with George and to have re-established the domesticity they had enjoyed together previously. Not domestic bliss, she accepted, but a life together where she felt safe and cared for. George was not perfect; that she knew. He had his bad points. In fact she struggled to find many good points in his favour at times, but he was not violent to her, and that counted for a lot after her early experiences in life. He always offered her a cup of tea when he made one for himself. He must be clever with money as he always had sufficient for their needs without being in any way flash. George didn't do flash as a rule. Not by choice anyway. His devotion to caring for Evelyn was complete without being a threat to Janine. He didn't look at other women when she was around and sleeping with Lola Cortez had been an unfortunate episode which was clearly that Spanish Slut's fault, not George's. As long as she could keep him in her sight she could keep him safe and point him in the right direction to be good partner.   In short she found him reassuring; comfortable in the way his favourite chair clearly was for him.

The holiday was a way for the two of them to cement their relationship and move forward together with no reference to any lingering issues regarding the recent separation. A week of calm, relaxed, even boring time with George would be the perfect springboard to their future together. At least there would be no chance of drunkenness, fighting or lusting after other women. Boring and easily influenced could be such attractive qualities in a man.

The couple rose early the first morning of their holidays to find the sun shining, the car already packed and both of them in a mood of almost childish anticipation. They kissed before sitting down to breakfast and held hands later as they walked towards the car. George had even put the toilet seat down after his usual lengthy visit. All in all things were shaping up well for a great and peaceful break which would hopefully be the start of a long future together.

Chapter Five - Remembrance of Times Past

The news of Stevie 'Spider' Webb's escape from a prison van was all over the news two hours after it happened. Partly this was due to journalists monitoring the police radio frequencies and the immediate postings on several officers' Twitter feeds but it had more to do with the fact that he was a clear and certain danger to the public and Police Scotland made a point of informing all media outlets using a prepared warning message straight away. The message warned the public not to approach him, but although it didn't say that if he approached them they should be afraid, very afraid, it did hint at it.

Prison life had not been kind to Spider and in turn he had not been kind to anyone who lived or worked in prisons. After only six months locked up in Glasgow's Barlinnie prison, he had attacked sufficient staff and prisoners and become so unreasonable that he had been certified and sent to the State Psychiatric Hospital in Carstairs. He had objected to this even more and his lawyer had found sufficient mistakes in the hastily prepared paperwork to represent realistic grounds for appeal. Technically no longer mad, Spider had to be returned to Barlinnie pending a full hearing in front of a High Court judge. This took two weeks to organise; a period as traumatic for the staff of Barlinnie as Spider now claimed Carstairs had been for him.

An early date was made available, during which a largely unsympathetic judge listened to all the available reports and concluded that Stephen Webb was in fact a dangerous psychopath whose rightful place of incarceration was not a mainstream prison but a secure facility with specialist psychiatric treatment, in particular a shed-load of drugs to render him docile. Stephen Webb violently disagreed and had to be forcibly removed from the court by four large prison officers, one of whom was subsequently hospitalised. Spider's strong objection continued on the return journey to Carstairs during which he attacked the escorting officers and somehow managed to escape when the van stopped to allow the escorting police to assist.

The violence meted out to those in Spider's way loomed large in all the news reports and the Police were keen to apprehend him for this reason alone. What they knew and what did not feature in any of the reports was the fact that a detailed search of his cell had uncovered a small collection of folded foolscap paper forming a diary of sorts. Each entry was dated and contained a violent rant in Spider's strangely neat handwriting. It was a diary of hate; hate directed at the system which had deprived him of his freedom. Most of all though, it was a diary of hate directed at two people: people Steven Spider Webb held responsible for his loss of liberty. The title page appeared to be written in blood and was a bit of a give-away regarding the book's subject matter.

It simply read: "George Milne and his bitch Janine must Die."

Chapter Six - Jimmy Bell's Legacy

Inspector Janice Young sat at her desk reading through the notes in Spider's file. There were annotations throughout in her former boss Jimmy Bell's hand writing. Time and again it was noted that George Milne had been interviewed and discounted as a suspect.

"George Milne interviewed at home. No longer a person of interest."

"George Milne source of evidence. No further action."

"George Milne interviewed under caution. Removed from list of suspects."

"George Milne handed over fingerprint evidence at his home. No further action."

The more she read the notes the less she could believe what she was reading. Jimmy Bell had met or interviewed Milne at least eight times during the course of two murder investigations, discovering key evidence which led to a conviction in each case. He had been seen in the area of Frankie Cook's flat at or around the time Frankie was killed, a day which also saw the violent death of Willie McBride and an ex-felon neighbour, and yet he had never been so much as questioned by Bell about it. He was in the Hotel carrying identical knives to the murder weapon when Eric Ramsay was stabbed to death and was released after she and Jimmy had interviewed him without charge and without any restrictions on his movements. As soon as the dust had settled from Jimmy's big drugs case, Milne had moved his step daughter, Rosie, into the very flat where McBride had been found dead and where Frankie had lived before failing to fly in the stairwell, falling to his messy death below. Since then Rosie and her girlfriend Carol had lived there with Frankie's sister, Evelyn.

A picture was building up in her mind which she found very disturbing. Milne was obviously guilty as sin and was in cahoots with McGovern, Rosie and Evelyn Cook but there was more. The only way Jimmy Bell could have missed this fact was if he chose to. In other words, for whatever reason, he had chosen to let Milne take over Frankie's patch. Bell wasn't the great detective his superiors believed him to be but he wasn't that stupid. Either Milne was paying him to look the other way or he had some kind of hold on Bell which was strong enough to manipulate his actions. Either way, Bell had to be a bent copper as far as she could see. He had been promoted and was now Detective Chief Inspector Bell with the Queen's police medal to boot. If she mentioned her suspicions to anybody it was more likely to finish her career than his.

She had to play this one close to her chest. If Bell or even Milne got wind of the fact that she had sussed their little arrangement she would be finished. She needed to be able to prove this to her superiors beyond any doubt before saying anything. She had to move things forward though and decided to phone Bell directly on the pretext of picking his brains on Milne and McGovern's whereabouts. It was a logical thing to do as officially Milne was merely an innocent member of the public whose life and that of his partner were in danger from a dangerous escaped murderer. She knew better though and Jimmy Bell might just slip up and give something away, incriminating himself in the process. Before that though, she would get somebody to bring in Evelyn fucking Cook who could maybe fake learning difficulties with others but not with her.

"Dixie," she said. "Bring this Cook girl into custody."

"What pretext Boss," he asked.

"Oh, let's just call it protective custody. Poor wee thing might be in danger from this Spider character too. While she's here though, I might just have a private chat with her and let her know we are on to her and her pal George Milne's game. Let's see if she has difficulty learning that fact."

Chapter Seven - Giving Jimmy a Bell

"Hello, Chief Inspector Bell?" said Janice.

"Hi Janice. I think you can call me Jimmy now. How's it going over in Coatshill?"

Jimmy sounded relaxed enough, Janice thought. Let's see what happens if I turn up the heat a bit.

"It was quiet, Jimmy but an old friend of yours just escaped and livened it up."

"If you mean Spider I don't think he has any friends," Jimmy laughed. "I saw he was on the loose. We have pictures out to everyone here too but he doesn't have any Edinburgh links as far as we know. I'm afraid he is more likely to show up on your patch."

"We think he might be trying to find your other friend here, George Milne and his girlfriend Janine McGovern. What's your take on that?"

"Sounds likely enough to me," said Jimmy without any hesitation or surprise. " Better keep a watchful eye on them."

"We would if we knew where they were. They haven't been seen at home for days; almost as if they knew Spider was going to escape and come after them."

Jimmy laughed at the other end of the phone.

"Janine's smart perhaps but Milne doesn't know what day it is without asking her first. You remember what he was like when we interviewed him about Eric Ramsay's murder? Anyway, how would they know in advance that Spider was going to escape?"

Janice knew he was testing her; he had to be, but he was keeping pretty cool about it all.

"You're right. It would have been as much of a surprise to them as us. Any idea where they might be?"

"Have you tried The Ranch Pub? It was where they met and last time I saw them that's where they were. If they're not there one of the locals might know."

"Thanks for that, Jimmy. I'll keep you posted. What about Evelyn Cook?"

Janice left the question hanging and was pleased to see that it seemed to throw Jimmy. There was a decided pause before he replied.

"What about Evelyn?"

He managed to sound as if he didn't understand the question, Janice thought. He was a cool one right enough. His voice didn't suggest he was frightened of anyone or anything. No, he had to be in it with Milne. She better play it cautiously.

"Oh I was just concerned Spider might come after her too. Was she not involved in Frankie's business too?"

Again Jimmy laughed.

"Evelyn makes Milne look like mastermind. I'm afraid she is completely Dolly Dimple and always has been. She has no idea what is going on around her. I can't see any reason for Webb to be interested in her. He may have worked for Frankie but he was never implicated in his death. Post a uniform outside the flat if you like but you'll be wasting your time."

"Okay. I just wondered if she had maybe taken over from Frankie in some way?"

Again there was a pause at the other end of the line. Janice pictured Jimmy starting to sweat at her line of questioning. For his part though, Jimmy was starting to have serious doubts about recommending Janice for promotion.

"Take it from me that Evelyn is an innocent victim of her brother's life of crime."

His voice was taking on the tone of a superior officer again.

"Find Milne and Janine McGovern before Spider does or you'll have two bodies to deal with. Trust me on that one."

Janice sensed the tone change but decided to push her luck one last time.

"I thought that Milne might be more than capable of looking after himself if they met up."

Again there was a pause as Jimmy wondered if it was too late to return Janice to the rank of sergeant and maybe desk duties somewhere quiet.

"Oh, if they meet up there will be violence right enough, but it will only ever go one way. Now I need to get back to catching Edinburgh's villains. Good luck!"

Janice heard the phone going down rather quickly at the other end of the line.

"What did Jimmy mean by that?" she wondered. He certainly seemed concerned that Spider was at large. Reading between the lines there were two ways she could take the conversation. Jimmy clearly wanted her to believe that everything was straightforward. Spider was a dangerous crook looking for revenge on the innocent members of the public who had helped put him behind bars in the first place. Find him and end the danger to the public: simples. But that was too easy. He had been adamant that Evelyn was the simpleton she appeared to be. Was he trying to protect her? After all she was still living in the hub of Frankie's old business. Somebody had taken over the Coatshill franchise after Frankie died and there were no definite leads on the files as to who it was.

Jimmy also wanted Milne and McGovern to be found and protected. If he was an accomplice of theirs it would make sense to protect his colleagues. But it was his last comment that had her most perplexed. What had he meant when he had said, "Oh, if they meet up there will be violence right enough but it will only ever go one way." Did he know something about Milne that she didn't? Maybe Jimmy wanted Milne found before he had to show his hand as a real villain. If that happened then Jimmy would expose himself to doubts about their relationship and his own potential guilt. Whatever happened in the hours and days ahead, she was sure that it would provide her with a deeper insight into what had really happened while Jimmy had been working in Coatshill. If she was right and Jimmy was a bent copper she would bring him to justice, whatever the consequences might be for her.

Chapter Eight - The Caravan Park

George had promised Janine a full week of his undivided attention and this extended to forgoing his custom of watching the news. It also extended to not listening to the news in the car on the way to the caravan park. Instead Janine had brought a selection of CDs, both hers and George's and they listened to them turn about as they drove. The relaxed mood of anticipation continued as they travelled and they were both looking forward to the break.

Had they popped the radio on for even one brief news report they would have become aware that Scotland's most wanted criminal was on the loose somewhere on the West Coast. Had George remembered to take his phone he would have received at least one of the urgent warning messages from Police Scotland. Had Janine not lost her old mobile phone and replaced it with a new one and new number the previous week she may have received one of the messages directed at her. Had they left details of where they were staying with Rosie or Carol instead of the enigmatic "surprise destination" description they may have had the warnings passed on. But none of these potential interruptions spoiled the journey from Coatshill to Ayrshire, nor put a damper on their expectations for the week ahead.

The sun continued to shine and the music enhanced their mellow mood. Janine had bought a CD of songs ideal for cruising around in a car, according to the packaging and they found themselves singing along to Cliff Richard's Summer Holiday among other more dubious cruising greats.

"We're all going on a... Summer holiday. No more working for a week or two," they sang and giggled away like children.

"We're going where the sun shines brightly..." they sang and giggled at the clouds in the west.

They stopped for a pub lunch on the way and the staff mistook them for newlyweds, such was the intimacy of their conversations and the way they held hands. They laughed, they kissed, they touched and Janine gently wiped away crumbs of food from George's face as they ate. Nothing was going to spoil this trip, Janine thought to herself. Nobody was going to come between them. Certainly not that Spanish bint from Drumchapel!

They arrived at the caravan site and found the touring area was well sign-posted. The caravan on the pitch wasn't the newest in the row by any stretch of the imagination but it looked wind and weather-tight and they were both too happy to care about anything else. They found the key hidden where they had been told it would be and opened up the door still smiling and giggling at each other. The smell of musty, slightly damp bedding hit them straight away and the smiling stopped. Although there was no obvious leak it was clear that the place hadn't been used for some time and that dampness had been allowed to pervade the soft furnishings and make them smell. They looked at each other but were still buoyed up by the warm feelings stemming from the recent reconciliation and were determined to let nothing spoil the break. Janine shrugged her shoulders and George did the same in support.

"Not to worry. I'll take the bedding to the laundrette we passed on the way in and you put the kettle on. Either that or open a bottle of wine," she said.

George felt the responsibility of choosing was too great for him. He made coffees and opened a bottle of wine after Janine had left with two bin-liners full of stale bedclothes. She had also hung out the duvets on a line near the awning attached to the caravan and it looked as if the holiday could be saved after all. George opened all the windows of the caravan which still worked and left the door open too. He was still in high spirits and sang away to himself as he poured two large glasses of red wine and placed them beside the cooling coffees.

"Fun and laughter for a week or two..."

The cupboards of the caravan had everything his cupboards at home had and more. The individual sachets of sugar suggested a branch of Costa Coffees had been left a sugar free zone and there were three different jars of coffee, all of them open.

"To make our dreams come true..." he sang to himself.

Janine returned and took both the wine and the coffee forward to the bench seats at the front of the caravan, giving George a lingering kiss as she passed. He joined her there and they watched other caravanners walk past and the children play on scooters and bikes along the pathways. Despite the screams and shouts of the children, it was a rather peaceful and reassuring scene. Janine left her coffee largely untouched but finished her glass of wine quite quickly. George got up and fetched the bottle from the galley, topping up her glass before he sat down again. George would have much preferred a good pint of beer and drank his wine slowly and reluctantly but it was nice to sit with Janine, keeping her company without a care in the world.

After an hour or so the bottle was empty and Janine was nearly asleep.

"The bedding will be washed by now," she said. "I better go and put it in the tumble dryer so it'll be ready for tonight. The smell seems to have gone from here now."

George realised she was tired and he was desperate for a pint and so he offered to go and sort the washing, suggesting she have a nap before they went for dinner.

"The bedding is in the first washing machine on the right as you go in," she said in a voice which confirmed sleep wasn't far away.

George put his coat over her and headed off to the main complex. He passed the laundrette and continued on his way to the bar. There he found a selection of beers including one of his favourite real ales and sat on a barstool near a television screen in the hope of catching a news bulletin. After a moment or two and a few sips of beer he realised the television was on a channel unique to the company which owned the site. Music videos were alternated with details of the park's attractions and adverts for the easy payment terms available for those wishing to buy a static caravan on the site. George was disappointed but only slightly as he was enjoying the beer.

When he had finished two pints he decided he had been away long enough and headed back towards the laundrette. he remembered Janine's instructions that their washing was in the first machine on the right as you went in the door but had missed the fact that the building had a door at each end and he was now returning from the main complex, arriving at the opposite end of the building. He walked in and sure enough found the first machine on the right had finished its wash cycle and that the door had unlocked automatically, ready to be emptied. He looked round and saw a row of five tumble driers further along the wall and opened the door of one of them, ready to smoothly transfer the bedding.

As he opened the door of the washing machine a hard-faced but rather attractive and very fit woman of 30 or so walked in and he smiled and said "Hello".

She said hello back and looked round momentarily disorientated. George opened the washing machine and reached inside. The handful of material he pulled out was not bedding as he had expected but was instead a bundle of ladies underwear and nightwear. George didn't think the lacy sets were Janine's and he put most of the bundle down and inspected a wispy red thong carefully to see if it jogged his memory. As he did so he became aware that the lady who had entered the building shortly after him had now fully regained her bearings and was staring at him as he assessed the underwear from the machine.

"I think that's mine," she said in what he suspected was a Newcastle accent.

"I wasn't sure," George replied before realising he had entered the laundrette from the opposite end that Janine had.

"My partner put our things in and I must have got the wrong machine."

The woman eyed him up suspiciously and after a moment nodded, putting her hand out to receive her favourite thong. George handed it over and was about to pick up the rest of her underwear when she told him not to bother. He turned and worked out which machine Janine had used, went over to it and started emptying the bedding items ready for tumble drying.

"Easy mistake to make," said George holding up a double duvet cover.

The woman looked at him, unsure which item of her lingerie he had mistaken for a duvet cover and just smiled a rather embarrassed smile. Maybe it was a genuine mistake, she thought to herself. Or maybe he was an ageing pervert right enough who had spotted her knickers in the machine and tried to steal them. She shrugged as George left, prepared to give him the benefit of the doubt but glad that her boyfriend Dean hadn't been with her. He might not have been as ready to forgive and forget.

George found himself vaguely thinking about the lady from the laundrette and her choice of underwear as Janine grabbed him and tumbled him into the bed shortly after remaking it with the freshly cleaned bedding. After they had made love George wondered what Janine's reaction would be if he bought her a wispy red underwear set with a particularly skimpy pair of thong knickers. He wasn't sure but resolved to find out on her next birthday in a few months time. If the charming lady with the neck tattoo had liked them then surely Janine would too. She might even fancy a neck tattoo to go with it.

Although perhaps that was a step too far.

When they had finished planning the rest of the evening they got out of the bed and went to the shower block to get cleaned up before dinner. They were both hungry and it was starting to get quite late. They walked hand in hand, and giggled when they had to separate at the two doors, one for Men and one for Ladies. They would have taken a shower together in the caravan if there had been room and the shower-head had produced clean water rather than a brownish sludge when they turned it on. Not to worry. They would be quicker showering separately, and ready for dinner earlier than if they headed naked into the intimate space of the caravan's shower. Who knows what might have happened once the sludge had cleared and warm water hit both their soap covered bodies in such a confined space? Who knows? Certainly George didn't as he enjoyed the endless hot water and ample space of the gents' showers. He was hungry and focused on a good meal with, perhaps, some more of his favourite beer to wash it down.

Chapter Nine - Mulligans

Cheeky Charlie Mulligan had been called up for World War Two and loved every minute of his four years in the Royal Army Service Corps. He loved the camaraderie of service life, he loved the uniform, he loved the girls who found uniforms irresistible, but most of all he loved the fact that he was never sent to fight the Germans or the Japanese. With a borderline heart murmur he had been medically classified as not suitable for front line service and was posted to the RASC where a brief aptitude test suggested his future lay in supplying blankets and supplies to UK barracks. This he did with great enthusiasm, realising early that his counting of supplies was assumed to be accurate by his superiors, even when the totals were below what they should be. Any surplus generated by his creative counting techniques, Charlie sold off on the black market, pocketing the salary equivalent of a full general for most of the war. When he was discharged shortly after VJ day, he invested in an expensive suit and lodgings and looked around for a suitable way of establishing a legitimate business. He bought several properties and rented them out but this lacked the excitement he was looking for. It just wasn't hands-on enough and was too slow a method of laundering his ill gotten gains from selling military laundry.

A year after the war, as returning servicemen settled down and started families or met the ones they had started before going overseas, Charlie realised that there was a gap in the market for holiday destinations for these newly formed family groups. Few could afford to go abroad and fewer wanted to but they wanted to get away from the humdrum lives they led for at least a week each year. Charlie also noticed that the War Office was selling off many of the surplus army bases which they no longer needed for the far smaller, peacetime army.

Charlie put two and two together, and bought six such camps around the UK which were more or less beside the sea. The first one was in Ayrshire and with a lick of paint and army surplus supplies he turned it into a cheap and cheerful holiday camp, complete with concrete swimming pool and tennis court. The first year he could have filled it twice over and emboldened by his success he refurbished another two of his camps in time for the following summer. Over the next five years he bought further former bases and developed them till he eventually owned 20 such holiday camps around the country. They became well known for sea, sand and illicit sex, if not always for sun. The bars were expanded from the original former NAAFI clubs to nightclubs with shows. Many famous entertainers got their first breaks at these clubs and many former army concert party members kept the false dream of stardom alive for years after being demobbed. They had the advantage of being run on almost military lines with participation in good times compulsory.

Charlie made a packet and became a household name. He was a working class hero to many who had worked his way up from scratch, as they saw it, unaware of his wartime sideline in stolen rations and clothing. It was through his hands-on interest in the dancing girls from his shows that he met his wife Carol "Ginger" Rodgers. She was beautiful with long dancer's legs and was Charlie's equal when it came to the money side of the business. Their romantic and business partnership blossomed and they had two healthy sons in the mid-1950s, both of whom grew to be lazy and incapable of employment outside the family business. Charlie and Ginger doted on them and lavished the material benefits they had both had to do without during the war.

The business prospered and the family grew wealthy. Charlie bought a huge mansion in Essex and began to visit his camps less frequently. As baby boomers' tastes changed and they demanded more for their holiday pounds, Mulligans holiday camps began to suffer. Charlie managed to diversify into other areas of the holiday business and used the profits from these ventures to subsidise the failing camps. Without such support, the camps would have closed by the 1970s. Instead Charlie managed to keep them afloat and even nurse them back to health as weekend destinations. He had had to reduce the number dramatically but had managed to sell all but six of them off to developers for a healthy profit as the baby boomers chased the dream of home ownership.

His sons watched the family fortune stagnate and found their parents' longevity a constant source of disappointment. Eventually, Ginger succumbed to a severe bout of pneumonia in the early years of the 21st Century and a heartbroken Charlie died the following year, having lost the will to carry on without her. On his deathbed, or at least the day before it became such, he had made his sons promise to continue the family business for the rest of their lives.

"The name and tradition of Mulligan's holiday camps must continue after my death," he said as they swore to honour his wishes.

They kept their promise for six months after his death, until they were approached via their solicitor by a multi-national travel firm which had an eye on their Spanish package tour subsidiary and the land around the remaining six camps which was crying out to be developed. After a short period of negotiation, the young Mulligans each pocketed around about 10 million pounds and embarked on easier lives than their father had anticipated, without a moment's thought to his dying wish.

Elysian holidays invested heavily in refurbishing their new holiday camps, adding water activity centres, golf courses, updated serviced static caravan plots and recreational facilities. The camps were rebranded as upmarket family holiday destinations for the "stay-cation" generation and they started to make money again. Television and radio advertising ran constantly at the start of each year, the second that people had finished the last of the Christmas turkey and thoughts turned to summer breaks.

Elysian, which had started as a time share operator marketing almost exclusively to the comfortably retired, had bought into a new generation of customers and the profits forecasts were exciting. Ten years later after the camps had again been established as desirable places to go and have fun, with or without the children, the parent company were happy that they had achieved what they had set out to do. Everything that is except persuade their customers to use the new name for the camps. As far as the happy campers were concerned it was still Mulligan's they went to. If Charlie was able to see this from whatever final resting place he inhabited he would have been delighted that the name and traditions of Mulligan's holiday camps had survived after all.

Mulligan's Holiday Camp Girvan had been one of Charlie's favourite camps, not least because he had actually spent time there during his national service. Ironically, he had gone there with the captain who was notionally in charge of his own unit to investigate the disappearance of supplies which Charlie quickly realised was down to the dishonesty of a clerk in the unit. The method of misappropriation was quite amateur in nature compared to both the subtlety and scale of Charlie's own efforts, and he was able to identify the culprit to his rather thick officer quite quickly and also to recover half the missing stock from a series of buildings on a farm nearby. Other items didn't make it back to war stocks as Charlie found himself left in charge of matters while the Captain spent his time fishing with a distant cousin on an Ayrshire estate in the area. Charlie made some money from selling some of the stock and from the farmer who had been in on the deal and didn't want to be prosecuted.

When Charlie was told to take his time and that they would not be heading back to their own unit for several days, which conveniently coincided with the end of the salmon fishing season, he used the staff car and the petrol to explore the area. It had some lovely sandy beaches which he used for picnics with the barmaid from the pub where he was accommodated. In all, he spent 10 happy days in the area and returned to his unit with cash in his pocket, a C.O.'s commendation, a love of Ayrshire and a rather worrying rash around his genitals.

When he managed to buy the camp and set it up as a holiday destination Charlie spent as much time there as he could. The camp was conveniently near the beach, which was sandy, and thus provided free some of the building materials he needed for developing his camps, until the Scottish Environment Protection Agency became alarmed at the loss of natural habitat.

When Elysian Holidays eventually purchased it they improved facilities dramatically. The pock-marked approach road was widened with a safe exit from the nearby trunk road and trees and bushes were planted extensively around the whole site to both screen it from the road and to enhance the image of Mulligan's Girvan. They also put the prices up accordingly which provoked a revolt amongst the regulars who formed a very successful campaign to restore prices to the level affordable by the families who had used it for decades. The campaign was aided by a number of celebrities who had holidayed there as children and the editor of a national newspaper who owned a static caravan there for holidays with his grandchildren.

Elysian relented and Mulligan's Ayr remained a more budget destination than some of their other camps, continuing to attract its traditional clientele from Glasgow, Lanarkshire and further afield amongst Scotland's city dwellers keen for home based sand, sea and fun for their families.

Chapter Ten - Spider on the Loose

After his escape from the prison van transporting him from the court, Steven Webb quickly flagged down an unsuspecting motorist who recognised the prison uniform a little bit too late. Spider leapt at the passenger door before the driver could speed away and jumped in. The look on his face suggested to the driver, a middle-aged woman who represented a sewing thread manufacturer in their Scotland and North East region of the country, that she would miss her next appointment. Her day was generally spent trying to persuade other similar ladies who ran craft or haberdashery shops that they could live dangerously and order just a few more items from the latest supplier's catalogue. It was a phrase she used on a regular basis.

"Go on, live dangerously, take a selection from our metallic range too."

Living dangerously had today taken an all too real turn.

"Do as you're told and you won't get hurt," said Spider reassuringly after telling her to drive.

"Do anything stupid and you won't make it home. Got it?"

Mary nodded. She got it.

Spider gave her directions, emphasising all the while that she should drive normally so as not to arouse suspicion. He turned her radio off and even put his seat belt on. This gave Mary hope that he might not be such a bad man after all but Spider was guarding against the danger of her hitting the brakes or ramming a tree and relying on her airbag to come off better than him.

No such thought entered Mary's head. Instead she concentrated on the thought: "This too shall pass, this too shall pass."

And pass it did. Spider got her to pull into a lay-by on a relatively quiet stretch of country road. Mary feared the worst. Was he a rapist, a murderer, a terrorist (even if he did wear a seat belt)? He was obviously an escaped criminal. She knew that from his clothes and could see part of a handcuff still attached to one of his blooded wrists. She had earlier dismissed the possibility that he was on day release.

After checking that there were no cars approaching from either direction, Spider ordered her out of the car.

"This is a company car," she found herself saying before she could stop herself.

"That's handy," said Spider. "But I prefer my own company."

He followed her to the inside of the lay-by which sat at the edge of a fairly steep gorge.

"Give me your mobile phone," demanded Spider.

She took it from her pocket and handed it over.

"Give me your shoes," he ordered her.

They were expensive and new and she hesitated.

"Give me your fucking shoes!" demanded Spider.

Reluctantly she took each one off and then watched in horror as he threw them over into the ravine. She leaned forward involuntarily to see where they landed and felt a fierce kick on her bottom which propelled her over the edge in the direction of the shoes. She tumbled for what seemed like an age through bushes and shrubs before coming to a sudden stop against a tree. Dazed but still conscious, she heard her car screeching away from the lay-by and knew that her sales trip was over for the day.

Spider sped back to the main road, judging that he would have at least 20 minutes before the lady could climb to the top of the gorge, even if she found her shoes and then raised the alarm. If she had been knocked out or killed he would have longer. Either way he knew that would be long enough to make it to a rail Park and Ride which he knew 10 miles away. He would quickly dump the car then steal another and hope the owner of that was away for the full day or longer. If he could get another three hours it would be enough to reach a holiday home he knew of, near which he had hidden some stores for just such an occasion. It was all going perfectly so far. He had even managed to put two policemen in hospital for a very, very long time. He loved it when a plan came together.

Chapter Eleven - Dodgy Electrics

On the second evening in the caravan during dinner, the lights suddenly went out.   George walked over to the switch and put it off and then after a pause he put it on again. The bulbs flashed brightly for a second or two then went out. They seemed to reconsider things briefly and came on again only to go off and this time stay off. George tried the switch again and realised there was no longer any power getting to the lights.

"I'll have a look at the main connection outside," he said and headed through the awning and round to the services connections, noticing as he did so that there was a large tear in the fabric towards the rear which represented a shortcut for the way back. There he quickly saw that the power cable connector was loose and pushed it back in. The weight of it, however, pulled the cable loose again and although the lights inside the caravan had flickered into life, they gave up as the cable slipped down again. George tried pushing the cable in again twice before conceding that it would not stay in place of its own accord. The connection was part of a low but substantial post and he realised that if he could find something to bind the cable to the post it might stay in place. He could not remember seeing anything suitable in the caravan but decided that his belt would do as a temporary fix until he or Janine could find something better or buy some string in the well stocked site shop. He undid his belt and wrapped it round the cable and post several times until it stayed in place.

"Sorted," he said to himself as he stood up and confirmed the lights had gone on and stayed on this time. He then headed round the canvas of the awning towards the door and what he assumed would be a warm thanks from Janine. As he rounded the corner though, his trousers slipped to his ankles in the finest pantomime tradition and he tripped and fell over. Picking himself up but only raising his trousers sufficiently to walk the last few steps, he looked up to see a couple staring at his Y-fronts. He wasn't sure in the darkness but thought the lady might be the one from the laundrette so he smiled and shrugged his shoulders.

Her large and heavily built boyfriend didn't look impressed and she dragged him away whispering something about "that's him, the one I told you about, remember, in the laundrette".

The boyfriend looked back as George shuffled towards the safety of the awning but could not see him clearly.

Chapter Twelve - Where is George Milne?

Spider arrived at the Park and Ride and was pleased to find several spaces empty, including two which he judged to be almost hidden from the view of the security cameras. He carefully parked Mary's company car in one of them and then looked around for something anonymous but easy to steal. Again he was in luck. Three spaces down he found an aging family car which had been left unlocked. No doubt one press too many on the remote as a commuter rushed for a train he or she was close to missing.

Once inside he made quick work of opening the steering column and hot-wiring the ignition. The engine spluttered a bit and there was a hole in the exhaust, suggesting the car was a little under maintained. For a split second Spider considered stealing another one instead. It would be ironic to be stopped by the police for a faulty exhaust as he drove a stolen car towards his intended murder victims. On balance though, he decided that the noise wasn't too bad and he was better driving off immediately rather than wasting any more time on-camera near Mary's car.

He headed slowly out of the car park then opened up the throttle as he reached the main road. The car made a worrying noise on the corners to add to the roar from the exhaust confirming his suspicion that it would fail an MOT test.

"How could anybody let their car get into such a dangerous state?" He thought to himself. "There are laws against that."

He drove for an hour and a half till he arrived at a group of lock-ups on the outskirts of Glasgow. The third one had had its door forced as he anticipated but when he opened it up he knew from the look of the floor panels that his hiding place had not been discovered. A few minutes later, using the tyre jack from the stolen car, he had recovered a box containing clothes, a large quantity of money, a gun and a knife. Beneath the box were two false number plates and three cans of spray paint. He quickly swapped the number plates with the car out of sight inside the closed garage and then spray painted the main panels of the car. He added a line down the side in a second colour and cleaned the gun while he waited for the paint to dry enough to drive away.

Inside the garage he managed to relax. He was now in very familiar territory, and the fact that his lock-up had been broken into confirmed that the area hadn't changed much since he was there last. His breathing was steady again and he thought through his progress so far. It had all gone remarkably smoothly. Even the first vehicle hijack had been the perfect victim. There was nothing worse than some have-a-go hero slowing him down. Instead Mary had been scared enough to do exactly what she had been told and would have taken plenty of time to climb back up the hill even if she had found her high-heels.

The car he now had was a common Ford and was old enough to blend in with the general traffic. He had painted it a rather dull blue to replace the silver it had worn since leaving the factory and had number plates which aged it a further four years, plausible with the wear and tear it had received from its current owner. He now had fresh clothes, money and a choice of weapons with which to wreak revenge on George Milne and his girlfriend. If he was lucky he would be able to make their deaths particularly slow and painful using the knife. If he was pushed for time or had to act quickly before recapture then the gun would suffice. After he had killed them he would head south and take it from there. He wasn't bothered what happened in the long run but before he went back to jail he was determined to ensure one thing:

George Milne must die.

Chapter Thirteen - Janice and Evelyn Confused

Evelyn had been left alone in the flat she shared with Janine's daughter Rosie and her girlfriend Carol. That was not entirely unusual as she would be safe there and wouldn't normally worry as long as their absence only lasted for a few hours. Rosie and Carol had gone out shopping in Glasgow for the day and had arranged for one of the neighbours to pop in and make sure Evelyn was okay. Shortly after the neighbour had called, leaving Evelyn some home baking to enjoy, the doorbell rang again. Evelyn thought nothing of it and answered the door. Instead of the neighbour she found two female police officers standing there.

"Evelyn Cook?" one of them asked.

"Frankie's not in," replied Evelyn automatically before remembering that her brother had been dead for several years now.

"He won't be back," she added.

"It's actually you we have come to see," said one of the officers. "Can we come in?"

Evelyn had been strictly trained by Frankie never to let police into the flat and was about to say no when the older of the two neatly side-stepped her and walked into the hallway.

"We wondered if you had seen Steven Webb recently?" she said.

The name genuinely meant nothing to Evelyn and she looked puzzled.

"Spider," added the younger officer.

Evelyn recognised that name as one of her late brother's friends who had been involved in the same business. Her understanding of what that business was and what Spider's job title had been was very hazy but Spider had always been nice to her, even playing cards with her from time to time while he was waiting at the flat between errands for Frankie.

"He's gone away," said Evelyn, remembering that George had told her Spider had been sent to prison for a very long time.

"He's escaped and we wondered if he had been in touch," said the younger officer as her colleague took an uninvited tour of the flat.

"Not with me, no," replied Evelyn. "Maybe he'll come and play cards again though."

The two officers looked at each other and shrugged.

"We think you might be in danger from Spider and thought you better come down to the station with us till he's caught. Just to be safe."

Evelyn looked confused and a little frightened. She wasn't frightened of Spider, he was a nice man who had played snap with her while waiting to see people for Frankie.

She was frightened of the police and their station in particular. Frankie had often warned her about the dangers of the police station: a building where many of his friends had been taken, never to return - well not for a while anyway. Now she was being taken there and didn't know if she would ever get out again.

"I need to stay here," she said, as decisively as she could.

"Expecting anyone, customers maybe?" asked the older policewoman.

"Rosie and Carol but they're not customers," said Evelyn. "Well, they are customers today in Glasgow."

The officers looked at each other and nodded. They had been briefed on Janice Young's basic suspicion that George and Janine had somehow taken over Frankie's business interests and were using the flat and Evelyn's inside knowledge in particular to their advantage. Armed only with this information and having no previous dealings with any of the people involved they suspected that Evelyn had just hinted at Rosie and Carol being on a trip to buy drugs in Glasgow rather than a shopping spree in Dorothy Perkins and River Island.

"Get your coat then, Evelyn, we'll take you to the station where you'll be safe and you can tell us exactly what your friends are buying in Glasgow as we go."

Evelyn took her coat off the peg near the door and wondered why these police women were interested in her flatmates' shopping trip to buy swimming costumes and summer clothes for an imminent holiday in Greece. Maybe as police officers they didn't get to shop very often and were just looking for ideas. Evelyn had looked through the Next catalogue in the flat with Rosie and had a good idea of her tastes.

"Maybe if you have pictures at the station I could point out what they were after."

Again the police officers looked at each other. If Evelyn was prepared to point out the girl's associates from a book of mug-shots then it could be really useful. If so then clearly she wasn't helping George Milne's gang voluntarily but was happy to help the police convict them to gain her freedom now that they had taken her safely into their custody.

"That would be really helpful, Evelyn, although it isn't a book we use nowadays. The pictures are all on a computer."

"Like online shopping?" asked Evelyn.

There was a pause as the police women looked at each other, a little puzzled but not wanting to put Evelyn off.

"Sort of, I suppose," said the younger one before radioing in to her boss that they had Evelyn in protective custody and she appeared willing to cooperate fully in identifying George Milne's Glasgow contacts who were meeting with Janine's daughter and partner at this very moment.

When Janice Young received the message from the two uniformed officers she smiled.

"Looks like your little arrangement is about to come to an end, George Milne," she thought to herself.

If Evelyn has seen Jimmy Bell at the flat talking about anything suspicious then he would go down with Milne and McGovern too. If that didn't represent a career-enhancing opportunity for her, nothing would. A hardened criminal and the dodgy detective who had protected him for years in one fell swoop; she could read the headlines in the newspapers already. With thoughts of further promotion in her mind she telephoned a colleague in Witness Protection to advise him that she just might have a candidate for his department.

Chapter Fourteen - Beach Fit; Photo Fit

At the station Evelyn found herself being led to an interview room which was prepared with a coffee machine and a laptop as well as a tape recorder and notebook. It all struck her as a very formal way of planning a shopping trip but Frankie had warned her that the police were a strange lot. She sat down and was offered a coffee by the police woman who had met her transport on arrival. Evelyn had never liked tea or coffee and asked for a glass of wine instead. After being told that that would not be possible she happily settled for an orange juice.

"Hello, Evelyn," said Janice in an overly friendly tone. "I've been looking forward to having a chat with you and I believe you are willing to help us."

Evelyn smiled back. "Yes, of course!"

She liked internet shopping with Rosie and if this woman wanted to look through some online options with her that was fine. They didn't seem at all scary the way that Frankie had made out, quite the reverse. They had even given her an orange juice.

"Do you know which part of Glasgow your flatmates are going to?" asked Janice after starting the tape recorder.

"Yes," said Evelyn. "They were going to start in Argyle Street. Rosie said that's where they would get the important stuff. After that anything was a bonus."

Janice nodded, a little surprised at the choice of such a public place for any purchase of drugs, but in a way it made sense to hide in plain sight. If there was any problem they had a good chance of using the busy shopping area to escape. She looked at the one-way mirror, knowing that Dixie was behind it and would pick up the information. He should be looking up any intelligence they had about dealers who operated in that area.

"Do you know who they were going to buy the stuff from?" continued Janice.

Evelyn paused for a second. She could maybe help with choosing items that Rosie and Carol liked but she had never been good at remembering the names of any of the shops they mentioned, even the ones Carol and Rosie had taken her to. She could remember some at random but none sprang to mind at that moment in time.

"Do you have pictures?" she asked Janice hopefully.

Janice smiled. The laptop had been turned so that Dixie could see the screen from his hidden location. As soon as Evelyn picked out anyone, he could check their record immediately. They had agreed that they wanted the big players if possible and were prepared to follow up the information with phone taps and surveillance over a period of time if necessary. She asked Evelyn to move round slightly and clicked on the link which Dixie had sent her of likely players in Glasgow city centre.

Janice clicked on the first thumbnail and asked Evelyn to have a good look. Evelyn smiled and turned to the computer. She liked this woman. Then she didn't. Instead of an online shopping site she found herself looking at the type of man Frankie had worked with.

"Does he sell bikinis?" she asked.

"Bikinis?" asked Janice, looking for any humour in Evelyn's childlike face. Janice knew the slang names of every drug out there or thought she did. Everything from 'Charlie' to 'Jellies' but bikinis was new to her. "Do you think he sells bikinis?"

"Well that's what Rosie and Carol were wanting to buy first. They wanted to buy ones with yellow polka dots, like the song."

Janice stared at Evelyn to see if she was taking the piss and found the same child's face staring back.

"They really have gone to buy bikinis then?" she asked, starting to suspect that Evelyn was indeed as limited as she made out.

"Yes," said Evelyn. "I don't think this man works at Dorothy Perkins or Next. He probably wouldn't get a job at Ann Summers either, which is where they were going after that, though they wouldn't tell me what they were planning to buy there. What kind of clothes are you wanting me to help with? I like bikinis with spots, don't you?"

Two minutes later Janice was back at her desk with Dixie while an unfortunate woman police constable was tasked with keeping Evelyn company while the search for Steven Spider Webb continued. Janice had had to promise to ask Spider if he wanted to play snap with Evelyn when she found him before she could get her to stay at the station without getting overly anxious.

"We may have misjudged Evelyn's involvement. I don't think she knows anything, except where to find spotted bikinis. We will have to focus on the other players; Rosie and Carol have to be in the frame now as they moved in to Frankie's flat as soon as he was out of the picture. McGovern too, but Milne has to be the kingpin, and if he is, then the only way he has stayed out of jail so far is with the protection of Jimmy Bell. Jimmy was cool as a cucumber when I spoke to him earlier; not like somebody who had been scared into helping a villain."

Dixie nodded as his boss spoke, hearing a fairly plausible explanation for the continued drugs trade in Coatshill after Frankie's demise. He was less inclined to accept that Chief Inspector James Bell was a villain. But it wouldn't have been the first time a police officer had prospered whilst a criminal associate did likewise, passing each other key pieces of information to forward their own careers.

"I phoned internal investigation but they were lukewarm to the task without hard evidence. I didn't mention any names but they got cold feet as soon as I mentioned the rank involved. Hard evidence or count them out, basically," continued Janice.

"How do we get that?" asked Dixie.

"You follow Jimmy Bell till he makes a mistake," replied Janice.

For the first time Dixie became uncomfortable with how things were developing. It was one thing to talk casually about the possibility of a senior colleague being crooked but it was quite another to start following him without higher authority. If it was anybody's job it was a job for Internal Investigation branch and they were right about not doing it without good reason.

"I don't think we should do that yet," he urged his boss.

"Don't wimp out on me now, Dixie. This whole thing smells bad to both of us and if Jimmy is in cahoots with Milne we need to stop him. The first stage of that is getting evidence to pass upstairs so they can take over. That's all we are doing here. In effect it is just old fashioned coppering but doing it against a bent copper. Pass everything else you are doing on any other case to Sheila and start following Jimmy tonight. If we're right, he may even meet up with Milne or one of his associates, and if he does we've got him by the short and curlies. He mentioned he was speaking at the police training college this afternoon at four o'clock; you can follow him from there."

"I don't know about this boss. We can't even prove that Milne is a villain yet. He may just be the overweight and boring middle aged man he appears to be."

Janice snorted involuntarily.

"Don't worry about on that score. If Spider finds him before we do then whoever is the last man standing is the biggest villain. If Milne is innocent he'll be toast. If he is the hardened criminal I think he is then Spider will be the one who comes off worst."

Chapter Fifteen - Sharon the Tattooed Lady

George had managed to avoid any of the more energetic activities at the park, largely by expressing an interest in swimming to get some exercise while they were there. Janine welcomed this as she always felt George could do with losing a few pounds. Part of the reason George wanted to go swimming was the fact that he knew Janine was not keen. She disliked both the smell and the crowded changing areas where, although screened by cubicles, you were always aware other people were getting naked nearby. She accompanied him on the first visit out of duty but thereafter left him to go on his own. Her one and only foray confirmed her worst fears as she jostled on a rainy day with a long queue consisting mainly of Glaswegians with large numbers of large children for the all too few changing facilities.

Thus George was able to show some effort to swim before giving up due to overcrowding and then head off alone to the pool at least once each day with Janine's blessing but without Janine herself. On these occasions he felt no such obligation to swim or even move around in the pool. In fact the warmer bubbling hot tub beside the main pool had a magnetic attraction for him, allowing him to soak for an hour or so and watch the world go by. Most of the guests at the caravan park were either Glaswegians, from Lanarkshire or from towns in the North of England. A lot of the more expensive caravans seemed to be owned by grand-parents of all ages who brought their grandchildren here for a break from their parents. They ranged in age from mid 30s to 80 or so, though the older regulars could have been great grand-parents. The children were either emaciated or overfed to the point of clinical obesity. The grand-parents varied too but most of the older ones looked healthy and seemed to be enjoying retirement.

The adults between the ages of 30 and 50 were also either massively overweight or clearly spent a lot of time in the gym. The orange tanned ladies were what Rosie and Carol would have described as Gym Bunnies, while their husbands tended to look like bouncers from particularly rough city night clubs. At the other end of the spectrum the fat families were, almost without exception, incredibly fat. In some families though, there was often an exception. Here there would be one young lad or girl who was emaciated in a way that made George feel the rest of the family must be stealing all their food.

The other feature of his fellow swimmers which George noticed was the prevalence of tattoos sported by every generation. George found himself reading the messages on the bodies passing by or which slowly sank in to the hot tub beside him. Some tattoos were easier to read than others for reasons of position on the body, the font which

71

had been used, or in many cases the expansion of the area of skin where the ink had been originally installed.

There were many which had been homemade and simply recorded the name of the man or woman's greatest love; a person's name for the ladies, usually a football team for the blokes. It wasn't always easy to read the message in one glance without it being obvious so George would try and steal a second view on occasions and this could lead to embarrassing eye contact. Despite this he found it became an obsessive interest.

One day while he was sitting in the hot tub, a lady of 30 or so with a fairly athletic, gym-honed body climbed down the two steps into the water, allowing George to have a brief view of a tattoo on her inner thigh. He managed to read the words "Don't mess with me I'm from..." before her lower body sank beneath the bubbles.

"Where does she come from?" George wondered. There was something strangely familiar about her but he couldn't quite place it. As somebody who had travelled as little as possible in his life he hadn't met that many people. Had it not been for Lola Cortez he would have been largely restricted to the local population in Coatshill and the ticket sales staff at the children's attractions he had visited with Evelyn. Perhaps *he* had never seen her before and probably he never would again but the tantalising question of the lady's origins started bothering him for no good reason. It was impossible to read anything below the waves and bubbles but the tub had a timed cycle which meant the waters were still for five minutes or so after each bubbly session. He decided that it might be possible to read the missing word when the water stopped and so he positioned himself to get the best angle when that happened, hoping that nobody else would climb in and disturb the water. The woman had smiled an initial greeting before a moment of realisation crossed her face and her expression became less friendly towards George.

In due course the bubbles died down and he stared at the lady's inner thigh through the water. The ripples made it difficult to get a clear view and he failed to read it during the first interlude. When the bubbles started again George used the initial motion which affected everyone to reposition himself to get a better view of the missing word on the inner thigh opposite him. The word was very close to the triangle of black bikini between the lady's thighs, an area which he would normally have avoided staring at too closely. But the burning question of where she came from drove him on to take greater risks than usual.

At the next spell of relatively still water he thought he made out a B at the start of the word but he couldn't be sure. So lost was he in his studies that he failed to notice the fact that his staring had come to the attention of the woman, who was not best pleased. Without waiting for the bubbles to start again she left the tub, giving George a stare which would have curdled milk. He missed it completely though as he was watching her upper legs closely in the hope that he could finally read her home town. Unfortunately she turned in a way which gave him no view of her inner thigh. Instead *he* had found himself staring with disappointment at her well toned buttocks.

The woman stopped at the top of the steps and looked back at George in the hope of embarrassing him. Instead she found him staring unapologetically at her bottom. She walked off in anger to find her husband, who was watching football in the main bar. She would have to be careful how she mentioned the incident to him though but she felt she had to, having recognised George as the same man she had found inspecting her red, lacy knickers at the Laundrette.

Chapter Sixteen - In the Bar

After she had dried herself and dressed, Sharon headed for the main bar to meet Dean. On the way, however, she decided that it would be a mistake to mention the middle-aged man who had been staring at her in the Jacuzzi pool. Maybe he had been short sighted or had water in his eye. There could be a million explanations for why he had appeared to be staring through the bubbling water at her crotch and she was still unsure as to how Dean would react. She was afraid that he would be less interested in the possible innocent explanations and would jump to the obvious conclusion that the man was a lecherous old git who was staring at his girlfriend. If that happened she was still not confident that Dean's violent temper wouldn't reappear and result in hospitalisation for the man and re-arrest for her partner. On balance then she decided to say nothing.

After George had been in the pool area for almost two hours and noticing that his toes and fingers were all very white and wrinkled he showered, dressed and rejoined Janine who had been reading in the caravan. They had a quick lunch before heading over to the main complex where Janine had a hairdresser's appointment booked. They parted with a kiss just outside the main bar where George had decided to have a few pints of beer while catching up on the news if he could. A lot would depend on which channel was being shown and whether the staff could change it if he asked them.

He found the bar busy but there was an unoccupied table near the window area, and he bought a pint and walked over to it. As he sat down he realised that the table opposite had a younger couple sitting at it and the lady was the attractive woman he had noticed in the bubble pool. She was obviously now dressed, wearing a low cut pink tee-shirt and a very short denim mini-skirt. George smiled at her but found his greeting frostily ignored. The man at the table was watching a football match which was showing on all the screens in the bar, which ruled out any chance of George seeing a news programme for some time. His mind and eyes wandered until he realised that the woman's denim mini skirt had risen up at one side and he could read part of her tattoo. This time he could just make out the first letter of the town where she was from. It was obviously a capital B. Beyond that, though he could read no more than he could in the Jacuzzi earlier that day.

"What towns begin with the letter B?" he mused. "Blackpool, Bolton, Bradford perhaps."

The couple were not talking which meant he had no clue from their accents as to where they came from. As he stared at her, the woman became uncomfortable and moved on her chair. The skirt rode up slightly more and George adjusted his position to try to read the rest of the town name. Was that an L after the B? He couldn't be sure. What he was sure of when he looked up was that the boyfriend was staring at him with undisguised anger.

"Are you trying to look up my girlfriend's skirt?" Dean demanded angrily.

George had been caught off-guard.

"Yes, but I was just trying to guess where she came from," he stuttered.

"What the fuck are you talking about?" exploded Dean.

Sharon was annoyed at George but was more concerned by the look on Dean's face. It was a look she had seen often enough before and she knew what it meant.

"Ignore him, Dean, he's just an old pervert. He's not worth getting into bother over."

Dean would have heard none of this in previous situations but he found the voice of both his girlfriend, anger management counsellor and the prison chaplain come to his rescue. All three seemed to be saying: "Steady, Dean. You can do this."

The coping lines which he had learned and practised came to his mind and he began to breathe slowly and deeply. After five minutes or so the crisis passed and he gave George one more warning look before returning to watch the football match.

"Well done, Dean," said Sharon. "I'm proud of you."

She too glared at George before taking a magazine out of her handbag and flicking through it.

Chapter Seventeen - Sharon and Dean

George and Janine were not the only couple who were taking a break at the caravan site in order to put past problems behind them. Sharon and Dean from Blyth in Northumberland were there for very similar reasons. No infidelity had been committed by either party in their relationship though. If there had then one or other of them would have been in jail for murder.

Their relationship had been a stormy one from the outset as high school sweethearts. Sharon had been a promising hockey player and gymnast while Dean had been a member of the school football team. He played in defence as he was a vicious thug both on and off the pitch. This had been tolerated at first in his junior years at school but as he got larger and his tackles or after-school fights became more violent, he was dropped from the football team for ill discipline or suspended from school for fighting, the headmaster being the referee in both circumstances. Dean didn't specifically enjoy hurting people but he did have a temper which made it inevitable as soon as he saw red.

As he grew up, his temper got him into more and more serious trouble. Long gone were his chances of playing football at any level. Not only were other teams reluctant to risk their players on the same pitch as Dean but it became difficult to find ten other people to play on his side. His long suffering girlfriend made sure he suffered too for any embarrassment she experienced in his company, and as they both began drinking to heroic levels, this became a more frequent occurrence.

Not only did Dean find himself up in court on several occasions but so too did Sharon, who, when drunk felt obliged to attack anyone unwise enough to pick a fight with her Dean. Blame and responsibility were unimportant to her once battle was joined, and once sober she found herself increasingly struggling to justify her actions, even to herself. On one appearance in front of the judge she came perilously close to a long custodial sentence but was given the option of counselling instead, with the one year sentence suspended only on condition that she dried out and found a way to avoid her weekly brawls as Dean's tag partner.

She was not initially keen to engage with the course but found it was run by a female ex-RAF physical training instructor who started by threatening to punch out the lights of Sharon or anybody else on the course who took the piss. Sharon had to admit the instructor looked like she could give Dean a run for his money and she kept quiet during the first session, assisted by a raging hangover. Thereafter the two unexpectedly hit it off and they found a common interest in the gym. Sharon had let herself go after failing to make it as either a serious gymnast or hockey player, largely thanks to her relationship with Dean, but with the help of her new friend she began to shed the weight she had gained and to tone up her body.

While Sharon was rediscovering the positive energy of the local gym and weaning herself off the booze, Dean was banged up at Her Majesty's pleasure in H M Prison Hull. There he initially caused as much trouble as usual whenever anybody wound him up but he found the time began to drag and the separation from Sharon, volatile as their relationship was, more of a struggle than previously. Maybe he was growing up. He was 31 when he went to Hull and with little good behaviour likely, the chances were that he would be 33 by the time Her Majesty had finished with him.

Coupled to this realisation was the tone of Sharon's phone calls and letters. Gone were the sympathetic rants against the people who had picked a fight with them or the system which had chosen to favour the victims rather than the perpetrators. Instead there was a calmer, almost evangelical tone throughout her communications, written or verbal. Listening to her, Dean felt that she had changed, and changed for good. At first he assumed that she had met somebody else: as he always did, he saw red and hospitalised two wardens and his cellmate who he actually quite liked. After he calmed down though he began to think through his life to date and what losing Sharon might actually mean for him. There was plenty of time for contemplation in solitary confinement.

Dean slowly came to a realisation that he had to make a change, that his life to date had not been everything it could have been. There was no religion involved, or influence from HM Prison Hull staff or inmates but the thought of losing Sharon had brought about a profound desire for a new way forward. He wasn't sure at first how to go about it but inspiration came in the form of a Governor's assembly when the prison chaplain took the opportunity of a packed dining hall to say a few words. Whatever the words were, Dean could not have remembered them later; he knew as he left the dining hall that the padre might be the man to talk to. He made a formal request to the warder on his landing to meet with the chaplain. Initially sceptical, the warder told him to "Fuck Off!" but when Dean persisted without any actual threats of violence he passed on the message through official channels.

The padre was at first delighted to hear that a prisoner had requested to speak to him but became more cautious when he heard details of Dean's past convictions and his behaviour so far whilst incarcerated. The arrangements for the meeting and the number of warders who would be present was another heads-up to him that things might not be straightforward, but he had the strength of his calling and went ahead with the meeting.

To all the staff's surprise and relief, especially the padre's, the meeting passed without incident. True, he was disappointed that Dean had not suddenly seen the light and found religion but he was pleased that he seemed to be genuinely keen to renounce his past life of violence, particularly during their discussion.

"You see Vicar, I've fucked up all my life," confessed Dean. "I don't mean to hit folk but they just wind me up, like. Know what I mean."

The padre nodded and checked his exits for the 10th time. "Go on."

"Well, if someone wants to pick a fight with me that's fine. They'll lose mind but up till now it's been no skin off my nose. More often skin off theirs, like," and Dean giggled briefly before returning to the matter in hand. "But now I've had time to think things through I realise it's not worth it. I lost my chance to play proper football. I was good you know."

The padre nodded, finding himself relaxing slowly but surely. He had worked in prisons long enough to recognise when inmates were using a meeting with him as a ruse for any other purpose or just to take the piss, as his wife put it. But he saw in Dean an earnestness which suggested a genuine desire to turn his life around.

"What position did you play?" he asked as a means of keeping the conversation flowing.

"Defender, me." said Dean. "Nobody got past me to score."

The chaplain occasionally played five a side with some of his youth group and didn't fancy Dean tackling him. The urge to kick the ball away to someone else on either team as Dean approached must have been overpowering.

"So when did that go wrong, do you think?"

A dark look came over Dean but for a change it seemed to indicate anger at himself rather than anyone else.

"I don't know, it just did. Me own fault, like. When I met Sharon I was still playing football, like. She wanted me to train less but I told her to fuck off. Pardon the expression."

The Chaplain shrugged his shoulders in a way that suggested, quite rightly, that he was used to such language.

"We started going to clubs like and getting bladdered. Well, I started missing games on the Sunday or showing up late and playing like shit. The team captain would tell me off, like, and I didn't take kindly to it, know what I mean?"

The Chaplain nodded again, sympathising with the team captain; poor bloke.

"He did it a couple of times in the dressing room in front of the rest of the team and I had to hit him, like. Then he would tell me I was dropped from the team so I hit him again. A couple of times the police were called; no charges pressed like, just to pull me off. When he said I was dropped from the team I showed up anyway. After a while I would show up but the rest of the team wouldn't. I think they changed the venue. I tried playing for other teams but they were scared of my style too, especially if I had a hangover and didn't fancy chasing the strikers for a full 90 minutes."

The Chaplain nodded. "Was drink a big factor, then, in your problems with the football team?"

"Yeh! Big time. That and hitting people, like."

The two talked on beyond the allotted half hour. The warders took the Chaplain's thumbs up as a positive sign and were relieved that they had not been called upon to subdue Dean, yet again. By the end of the meeting the two men had come to an agreement to work together.

Although he wouldn't have used the same language, the Chaplain was prepared to help Dean to "unfuck his life", thus safeguarding his relationship with Sharon, unmarried as they were.

A further meeting was arranged, at which a definite roadmap to normalcy was agreed upon. The two would meet weekly to begin with and Dean would attend anger management classes held within the prison. If this went well, the Chaplain had agreed to meet Sharon and bring her up to speed with Dean's progress and commitment to change.

The weeks passed and Dean knuckled down to his task, making great progress. Attacks on staff and other inmates, both verbal and physical, stopped almost overnight. Messages relayed back from Sharon confirmed she was proud of him and that her time in the gym would make their future sex life together worth the effort for him. The prison chaplain was more comfortable passing the first of those messages to Dean than the second, but he felt close enough to the two of them by then and felt that this incentive was all part of the package. He had managed to resist Sharon's suggestion that he felt how firm her buttocks had become on a regime of one thousand squats a day but he was able to confirm to Dean that his girlfriend was very fit in the traditional sense of the term and that he knew this from visual evidence alone.

Months passed and staff were impressed with the way Dean behaved. He would be polite with them and managed to resist the efforts of some of the braver inmates to wind him up. Reports were written in terms which would have seemed impossible during the first six months of his sentence, and to everyone's surprise he became eligible to be considered for parole. On his second application, the parole board found no reason to refuse his application, try as some of them might, and he was released under licence and into the waiting arms of a transformed Sharon. Dean was left in no doubt as to his lonely future if he ever so much as threatened anyone again.

After the first week or so of passion they decided that a short break would be the ideal way of celebrating their new life together. As Dean had a lifetime ban from most places near their home town and due to the limitations of the parole requirements, they decided to head north of the border to Scotland where the prison chaplain had a static caravan. The venue had the added advantage that nobody was likely to recognise them or bear a grudge from previous altercations. Having once more sworn to his beloved Sharon that he was a reformed character and nothing could provoke him to his previous violent ways, they headed off for what they both felt was a well earned break.

Chapter Eighteen - Blue on Blue

Dixie was anything but happy about being tasked to follow a senior policeman on the mere say-so of his boss, a newly promoted Detective Inspector. As he drove to The Scottish Police Training College at Tulliallan, he started formulating career-saving excuses if he was caught. Most of these boiled down to the age-old formula of blaming his immediate superior. "I was ordered to follow him" sounded pretty weak, but it was true. He may have initially agreed with her assessment of Milne's activities and of Jimmy Bell's actions as his likely protector, but they were very short on actual facts to back up their suspicions. On the detective's course at Tulliallan he had been trained to be more rigorous than this. As he approached the place itself all the lessons came back to him and weakened his resolve. Just as he was swithering about turning round and trying to persuade his boss to think again, his mobile rang.

"Young here," said Janice. "I've found a note in Bell's own handwriting stating that he visited McGovern and Milne at The Ranch after Spider and the others were put away. He put a voucher through to buy flowers for McGovern though god knows what was inside them. Very careless, if you ask me, but it places him with them immediately after Frankie's demise. Stick to him like glue Dixie. If he slipped up once he'll slip up again."

The line went dead before Dixie could argue. He wasn't at all convinced that an expenses voucher for £30 of flowers proved anything. On the contrary, if Bell had put the voucher through it suggested the meeting had been innocent, or at least had nothing to do with dodgy dealings at the time. Having said that, his boss was even more determined that he follow Jimmy Bell, and arguing against it would clearly have set him at odds with the person writing his next confidential report, his first as a detective sergeant. Whatever else was true, arguing with Janice at this moment would have been detrimental to his long term career prospects.

Dixie drove in through the gates of Tulliallan, still with misgivings, but resigned to carrying out his boss's orders and with every intention of blaming her if it went pear-shaped.   He parked *his car* in the same car park as Jimmy's car, which Janice had identified for him, and opened his book while he waited for him to appear. As he had learned, most police detective work was about waiting patiently but alertly for the expected activity, and it looked as if the next day or so was going to prove this true, yet again. He almost missed the moment, so caught up was he in the Jack Reacher novel he was reading. Jimmy was in his car and leaving the car park before Dixie looked up and realised it.

He quickly threw his book onto the back seat, losing his place as he did so, and headed to the gate, worried he would miss which direction Jimmy took. In retrospect this was an unnecessary fear as turning left towards Edinburgh took in almost every possibility for central Scotland and a possible meeting with George Milne.

Turning right for the North took you nowhere, as far as Dixie was concerned.

Dixie followed at a generous distance, acutely aware that getting caught before finding anything incrimination about Jimmy Bell would be disastrous, even if he could shift the bulk of the blame to his boss. Jimmy headed on at a leisurely pace towards Edinburgh, oblivious to the fact that he was being tailed by a fellow police officer from the west of Scotland, who was there on the orders of a former protégé of his who was convinced he was in league with Lanarkshire's most dangerous criminal mastermind; George Milne.

Chapter Nineteen - Contact in the Pool

After his first encounter with Sharon in the Jacuzzi George decided to make it a daily or even twice daily activity in the hope that he would get a chance to read the final part of her tattoo. In pursuit of this information he found himself spending longer and longer in the hot tub each visit. As he reassured himself, even if she never reappeared, lazing around in the hot water could only ever be a relaxing and peaceful experience. What could possibly spoil an experience like that?

George was relaxing in the Jacuzzi one day hoping that nobody would disturb him with the possible exception of the lady with the mysterious tattoo on her inner thigh; purely so that he could finally determine where she was from.   He had gone during the children's Penguin Club daily show and it had paid off. He had the bubbly tub to himself although the two pools were full of mainly elderly swimmers swimming length after length at speeds that suggested they knew their peace would be shattered by screaming children all too soon. He felt the soft bubbles caress his body all over and felt a deep sense of relaxation flow, water-like with it. He and Janine were having a lovely break together which included just enough time apart to make it perfect. They had made love (twice), enjoyed good food, good beer and removed most of the stale smell from the caravan. Life was good, he concluded.

Considering the children's Penguin Club was in full swing in the show bar, George was surprised when a mother and two primary age children joined him in the pool. Surprised and hugely disappointed. They were followed uncomfortably quickly by two other ladies who were obviously part of the group but seemed unlikely to be related to the mother and children. One was a similar age to the young mother but was of Asian origin and the other was a very large woman, older than the other two but with no resemblance to either, ethnically or otherwise. The large woman was clearly uncomfortable in a swimming costume and immersed herself under the water as quickly as she could, a movement which resulted in her feet briefly linking with George's. The young Asian lady was equally uncomfortable in a one piece swimming suit which George recognised as one of the style for sale at the pool reception area. It was a rather strange group which seemed unlikely to decide to go swimming together.

The children spoke with broad Glaswegian accents to each other. But not, when they spoke to their mother, which they did in an Eastern European language unrecognisable to George. Whenever they did, the elderly woman translated everything they said to the young Asian lady whose name turned out to be Rowena. The elderly lady was called Melina and although she spoke the same language as the young mother, the way the two conversed suggested a formal acquaintance rather than any family tie. The children were clearly desperate to get back to the children's club and continually said so in both languages, one set of complaints translated each time by Melina.

As the mood of the group got worse and worse George decided he would leave but found his way to the steps blocked on one side by the large form of Melina and on the other side by the now badly behaved children. Instead he did nothing and hoped they would all go away and leave him in peace sometime very soon. They did not seem to notice him and their visit to the pool became more and more confrontational. The children began to plead with Rowena to go and join their friends at the children's club but she was adamant that they had to stay with their mother for another hour.

Why on earth would anyone force children to endure this experience rather than *the* Penguin *Club*? They should call social services or Child Line, George thought to himself. The prospect of being stuck in the hot tub with this strange group for a full hour persuaded him to leave but as he did so Melina slipped off the seat and her legs caught his, pulling him briefly under the surface. He struggled back to his seat and watched Melina do the same, releasing a large, bubbly fart as she did so and setting the children off into a fit of the giggles. She apologised to George in her native tongue before repeating it in English for his better understanding, giving the impression that she must live her life saying everything twice in two different languages.

He smiled and said it was okay, allowing Melina to return to her task of translating everything the mother or the children said for the benefit of Rowena.

Rowena seemed cross that the mother had taken the opportunity of Melina sinking beneath the bubbles to say something to the children. With no immediate translation available Rowena seemed concerned to discover what had been said. She repeated the words as best she could to Melina who looked blank then suggested a possible translation. At this the mother, who obviously spoke reasonable English, argued in her native tongue with both women, occasionally breaking into English to deny saying what they believed she had.

George was mystified and by now desperate to leave the hot tub although part of him wanted to see what happened next. The mother said something which was translated as her requiring to go to the toilet, and she left the pool giving George an angry stare for no good reason as she went. After all, he had been there first and would have already left if Melina hadn't sabotaged his efforts.

Once she had gone the children began demanding in English that they be allowed to go to the children's club and leave their mother behind. The other ladies again confirmed that was not possible as they had to spend another 32 minutes with their mother whether they liked it or not. The kids started splashing each other, and occasionally George, leaving the two women in peace to argue between themselves as to who had chosen the swimming pool as a venue.

"I told you the swimming pool was a bad idea," said Melina in her strangely accentless English.

"It was not entirely my decision," Rowena defended herself. "It was decided that the children might bond better with their mother if they interacted during an activity such as swimming. This is a first attempt so we need to let it run its course before evaluating its success."

"Or failure," added Melina angrily.

"Or if it is less successful, yes," replied Rowena.

"Why can't your mob just use the word failure?"

"There are positives in every situation," countered Rowena.

"What fucking positives are there in me looking like a beached whale and you christening a new swimming costume in this shit-hole just so that these kids can spend a tortuous hour with their mother, who they never want to see again?"

The children had stopped arguing and were looking at Melina, whom they obviously didn't like any more than their mother.

"You swore," said the girl. "You said the F word. I'm telling."

Melina realised her mistake and flushed red. Rowena tried to defuse the situation as best she could by suggesting the girl had misheard what had been said, before giving up and telling her that the word could have been mis-spoken. The kids were unconvinced, but to the women's relief though not George's, they went to back to squabbling rather than pursuing the bad language any further. The squabbling turned to physical violence which extended to kicking each other under the water, an activity which resulted in George's legs getting kicked more often than either of the children.

"Stop that immediately," demanded Melina before sliding under the surface again and once more releasing a huge burst of bubbles from her swimming costume.   When she made it back to her seat, the children were laughing at her, which at least had stopped their fighting. Rowena was trying not to laugh and told them to behave for the sake of their mother, who apparently only got to see them once a month. Melina slipped again on her seat which was far too small for the size of her bottom and she clearly was not used to sitting in a Jacuzzi or perhaps ever visiting a swimming pool at all. This time as she caught George's legs he managed to stop himself sliding under but only by splaying his legs and catching Rowena unawares at the knees. This time she slid forward on her seat and went under the water for a brief moment. When she surfaced her immaculate hair do was no more. Her make-up had not taken well to the soaking and mascara had started to spread around her eyes. She was livid at both the children and George.

"Would you kids behave !" she shouted, giving a look which seemed to include George .

"We want to go to the Penguin Club. This is boring."

"You'll bloody well stay here and like it," said a bedraggled Rowena before she could stop herself.

"You used the B word," said the boy, and his sister joined in.

At this point the mother returned, having used the 15 minute break to make a call on her mobile to her boyfriend. She seemed rather pleased that the children had been causing havoc in her absence, and giggled at the sight of their social worker. As she got back into the pool the movement set Melina off and she bobbed under the foaming bubbles once again. Everyone else laughed as she surfaced, with the exception of George, who tried to look uninterested in the whole group. Why anybody thought a trip to a swimming pool for supervised contact would be a good idea was a mystery to him and by now both Rowena and the interpreter Melina would privately have agreed. He suspected their swimming costumes would remain unused for a long time after this.

He managed to make it to the steps and leave before anybody else started arguing, fighting or sinking and as he walked away towards the showers he heard a brave Rowena try to refocus the session.

"Let's make the most of the last 10 minutes, shall we?"

"We want to go back to the Penguin Club ...ooooohhh, Melina farted again!"

Chapter Twenty - Jimmy is Tailed

Jimmy Bell drove back from his presentation to trainee detectives at Tulliallan rather disappointed. He had been asked to speak to the class because of his success on a number of high profile cases, most notably his disruption of Frankie Cook's and Jim Symons' gangs in the west coast along with the successful prosecution of Lord Strathbole for murder. He had put other villains away, but these were the cases which had made his name and established *his* reputation as a great detective who could solve crimes others might struggle with. Bell had traded on this reputation often enough at annual Confidentials and with his colleagues and had rather hoped to be treated with respect and perhaps awe from the students on the course. Instead he had found them hungry for knowledge and advice and thus rather dismissive of some of the answers he had provided.

He also had the distinct feeling they were generally brighter than he was. He had decided while preparing the talk that there was no need to emphasise the part which George Milne had played in either case, handing over vital evidence at key moments. Like all good detectives he wanted to keep his sources secret, but it did rather leave questions unanswered regarding how he had solved those cases. The young detectives seemed determined to get the details from the great man and the open questioning techniques they were being taught on the course caught him out more than once. By the end of the presentation he had become angry and had had to silence some of the more persistent of the, mainly, graduate students, by pulling rank and as a result many of them left the lecture room unimpressed.

Jimmy drove towards his house in the outskirts of Edinburgh annoyed at both the lack of respect he had been shown and the fact that he had handled the questions badly. It had not been a successful visit all round and he knew it. More to the point, the next generation of detectives knew it too and some had even hinted at the possibility that his key results owed more to luck than his abilities as a detective. "Cheeky Bastards" was the kindest way he could think of to describe them. Although usually awake to the possibility of some vengeful villain following him whenever he drove, on this occasion he was so engrossed in the failures of his presentation that he was completely oblivious to Dixie's attentions some 300 metres behind him all the way home.

Dixie pulled up far enough along the street where Jimmy Bell lived to be out of sight of the driveway where Jimmy had parked. There was only one narrow entrance to the garden and Dixie could see it if anyone drove out. He calculated that it was unlikely Jimmy would risk sneaking over the garden fence and use a neighbour's property as a means of escape. From the lace curtains and nosey gardeners trimming already immaculate hedges, it would be difficult for any such activity to go unnoticed. Either way, Dixie was on his own and could only cover the most obvious route in or out of the property.

He waited a few minutes, just in case Jimmy was merely collecting something important from the house and then heading for a meeting with one of the Milne Gang, and then phoned Janice.

"He's home from the Police College now; will I call it a day and come back early tomorrow?" he asked with more optimism than he felt.

"No chance. Until Milne or Spider are caught you stick with him day and night. We can't risk missing an opportunity to see them together."

Dixie was about to argue that it could be a while before any of that happened, if indeed it happened at all, when the line went dead.

"Bugger," he said loudly enough for an elderly dog walker to overhear and tut disapprovingly. Dixie wouldn't have been surprised if people in this part of town phoned the police to report language like that.

Chapter Twenty One - Jimmy Bell's Secret

Dixie was preparing himself for a long and cold evening when Jimmy reappeared driving his car out of the driveway at speed in the opposite direction to the one from which he had arrived. Dixie quickly switched on the engine and sped after him, concerned from Jimmy's speed that he might have noticed the tail he had acquired and was now determined to lose it before arriving at a clandestine meeting. In this respect, Dixie was partly correct but not in the way he then thought. Dixie managed to catch up with the other car but only just; the twists and turns it took within the residential area seemed to confirm that Jimmy was taking evasive action in order to throw him.

What Dixie could not know was that Jimmy had returned home still in a foul mood, only to be reminded that it was his turn to take their daughter to her ballet class some five miles away across the city during the rush hour. He had quickly lost an argument and abandoned his plan to have a shower, followed by a drink and a relaxing evening trying to unwind from his bad experience with the police cadets. Swearing under his breath at his wife and life in general he had smiled unconvincingly at his daughter as she took an age to get ready and then realised he was going to be very late for the class if he didn't get a move on. He was even tempted to use the blue light which was fitted to his otherwise unmarked car but refrained, aware that disciplinary action would almost certainly follow its use merely to get his daughter to her ballet class on time, if it ever came to light. He went through several amber and even one red light as he headed to the dance studio, oblivious to Dixie's struggle to keep up with him some five hundred yards or so behind.

"Shit," cursed Dixie. "He's on to me."

The two cars made as rapid progress across Edinburgh's traffic as they were able to, Jimmy in the lead, cursing and jumping lights with Dixie taking even greater risks behind him. They covered the three miles in what most commuters would have considered miraculously good time, but from the language in both cars you would never have known. Jimmy hit the brakes outside the dance studio so hard that he skidded, almost hitting the back of another parent's car already parked in front of the building. He swore loudly enough for his seven-year-old daughter to hear and give him a row.

He looked at the car's clock and realised he had just made it in time for the start of the lesson.

"Sorry sweetheart," he said to his daughter as he jumped out and opened the door for her. "I'll see you here in an hour."

?"But Abby's mum is collecting me and we are going to MacDonald's for tea. Don't you listen to anything I tell you when you're driving?"

'Obviously not,' Jimmy thought to himself.

"So you won't need me to collect you after the class, then?" he confirmed.

"Of course not, silly," said his daughter before running inside to join her friends.

Once back inside his car Jimmy breathed out slowly and whispered, "And relax."

Dixie pulled into the side of the street when he saw Jimmy hit his brakes and also nearly hit the car in front. He looked at the building and wondered why it had been chosen for a meeting with Milne, if that's what was happening. As he struggled to read the sign on the front door he saw Jimmy leap from the car and was about to jump out and give chase on foot when he saw the back door being opened and a small child jump out dressed in a tutu. She had been so small that he could not see her during the chase across town. She seemed to give Jimmy a mouthful and then ran up the steps of the building.

"Shit," thought Dixie. "He's just taking his daughter to a dance class. What a waste of effort."

Chapter Twenty Two - Jimmy's Bit on the Side

Jimmy had managed to relax and lower his blood pressure when his phone rang. He looked at the number of the caller, expecting his wife to phone and check that he had made it on time but it was not his home number. No, it was a far more welcome call.

"Hi you," said Jimmy in a warm tone his wife wouldn't recognise from recent conversations. "I wasn't expecting you to call for a while."

"I wondered if you had time to visit me sooner than planned. I'm missing you," said a woman's voice at the other end of the line.

"It's funny you should phone now. I just happen to have a few hours free. Is it too soon if I pop over now?"

"Not at all. The front door will be unlocked and I'll be hiding somewhere in the house. Do you have your handcuffs with you?"

"I never go anywhere without them," replied Jimmy.

"Good because I've been bad; really bad and need to be dealt with. Don't take too long."

The call ended and Jimmy put his mobile down on the passenger seat. Today might just turn out to be a better day than he had anticipated.

....

When Jimmy had arrived in Edinburgh as a newly promoted Detective Inspector he had found the desk work he had to do tedious and took every opportunity to get out and about. He called it "meeting the troops" when he accompanied his subordinates to crime scenes and to witness interviews. They called it "getting in the fucking way," but never to his face.

As a result of this policy, he found himself one day accompanying one of his detective constables to the scene of a break in and meeting the rather attractive and very recently divorced victim. Early on in the process of ascertaining what had happened and what was missing, the young DC got a phone call which was clearly from his wife.

"I can't go now," Jimmy heard him say. "I'm at a crime scene with the boss. Well, one of us has to collect him from nursery."

Jimmy's detective skills allowed him to figure out that his junior colleague had a small child at a nursery who was unwell and had vomited over one of the staff. He also concluded that his wife was a nurse who was working on a short-staffed ward and could not leave her post. Looking at the victim of the break-in he decided that perhaps this once, he could allow his colleague to have a few hours unscheduled leave to sort out his domestic problem.

Jimmy convinced himself that it would be the right thing to do, could safeguard the young officer's marriage and would allow him to demonstrate that his basic policing skills were still sharp.

"Billy," said Jimmy. "If you need to get your son from nursery, on you go. It isn't easy balancing two careers when you have a crisis like this, I remember it well. Off you go and I'll take care of this case. You don't need to mention it to anyone else."

Billy was surprised and very grateful to his boss and headed off, informing his wife on the phone that he had it covered. Jimmy rather hoped that his colleague would mention it in the canteen and establish a reputation for him as a caring superior. Either way it left him alone with a young woman who needed comforted by an authority figure. Perhaps someone just like him.

Jimmy noticed that Marion, the victim of the break-in, had been impressed by his kindness to his junior colleague. He smiled and shrugged as if to say "I'm a big softy really," and continued to take the details of the house and the losses she had suffered. Over the next two hours he discovered that she had recently lost some antiques, some mildly valuable jewellery, a large screen television, her mountain bike, a waster of a husband, the contents of their joint bank account and her best friend from school days who had taken a shine to him. Jimmy also learned that she was lonely, liked policemen, in or out of uniform, tall men, hadn't had sex for six months and owned a water bed. Jimmy managed to solve most of these issues while he was there with the exception of the identity of the perpetrator of the robbery.

It was more than professional courtesy for him to stay in contact with Marion after that and they began an affair which consisted entirely of regular sex every other Monday in the mornings after Jimmy had tasked his team and briefed his own boss. He left the police station under the cover of his "meet the troops" policy and none of them seemed to realise that they all had peace to get on with the job, every other Monday.

It was a surprise then when Marion phoned him late in an afternoon, during a week where they would not normally have met up. It had happened a few times and often Jimmy had had to decline the invitation but today, with his daughter's transport home already organised and his wife at the gym he could happily visit Marion for a little bit of extra-curricular activity which would, at her insistence, include the now rare use of his issue handcuffs. He sped off on the journey across town, still oblivious to Dixie's car following him all the way.

Chapter Twenty Three - A Dirty Weekend

Jimmy arrived at the tenement block where Marion lived, having parked his car a discreet distance away round two corners. This precaution on his part ensured that Dixie had to follow on foot at a safe distance, although he speeded up when Jimmy entered the communal entrance, in order to find out which of the eight flats he was visiting. Once he was sure Jimmy had gone in and, assuming he would be there for a while, he nipped swiftly up and noted the name on the door before quickly exiting the block and taking up position in a trendy cafe across the street. There he telephoned Janice.

"Hi Boss," he began, still a bit breathless from his climb to the third floor and back. "We might have a bit of progress here. Jimmy is visiting a flat near the town centre while his daughter is at ballet class. He went there pretty swiftly after receiving a phone call. I suspect something has come up."

"Good work Dixie," said Janice, jotting down the name and address but not recognising it from any of the files she had been studying. "I'll run it through the computer and see what I come up with, then phone you back. You stick with him and let me know when he leaves."

The phone went dead and Dixie was forced to order a coffee which his bladder could have well done without.

Jimmy Bell entered Marion's flat to find a note pinned to the wall opposite the front door and nobody obviously in sight. The note was scrawled but legible and said;

"I have been very bad and am now in hiding trying to resist arrest. I won't come quietly and will need to be restrained."

Jimmy's eyes lit up and he stripped down to his underpants, attaching his handcuffs to the elastic and began a thorough search of the flat in what had become a regular piece of theatrical foreplay. He found Marion hiding under the bed in the spare room, wearing only a lacy pair of knickers and matching bra. He gently but firmly pulled her out from under the bed as she protested her innocence of any crime and then led her to her own bed where he handcuffed her to the bedpost. The next half hour or so followed a tried and tested formula for eliminating any sexual frustration either of them had felt at the start of the meeting.

Afterwards while Jimmy showered and Marion made a pot of filter coffee, they talked about various things: politics, life in general, TV programmes they both watched separately but anticipated discussing on such occasions and even the weather. They both sat and enjoyed the coffee with chocolate biscuits, another guilty pleasure Jimmy was denied at home. He found he could hold a conversation with Marion in a way he never could with his wife. In part this was due to the busy nature of their lives together, forever taxiing children to activities around the city while working long hours to maintain careers which each of them felt worthwhile. But there was more to it than that. Marion listened and seemed to actually be interested in what Jimmy said.

Jimmy was brought back to earth when Marion said, "Why don't we run away together?"

The change of subject from the new US President to the suggestion of a naive bid for freedom caught him by surprise.

"I... I... thought we had agreed that... eh..."

"Oh I don't mean forever silly. I mean just take off for a few days somewhere where nobody would know us. Just for a change of scenery, rather than always meeting here in my flat."

"Oh I thought for a second you meant... Anyway I suppose we could - just for a few days." Jimmy said it vaguely as if he was buying time but the more he thought about it the more he liked the idea of spending quality time with Marion. The sex was good but he also looked forward to just talking and this could be difficult when time was short. He found himself adding: "When were you thinking about it?"

"I can make it pretty much anytime that you can get away. My parents have a caravan on a site in Ayrshire which they never make it to now so we could go there. My father had a stroke last year and my mother doesn't drive so they can't use it unless somebody takes them. They keep trying to persuade me to use it."

"A dirty weekend in Ayrshire?"

"Don't call it that. I prefer to see it as a romantic break."

"Maybe we could," said Jimmy warming to the idea. Neither he nor his wife had any relatives in Ayrshire and there was a fighting chance they could spend the weekend in complete anonymity. He regularly had to be away on business one way or another and it should be easy enough to come up with an excuse to be away again. His wife had always accepted it as part of his job, but recently he had sensed they both looked forward to such occasions. If anybody saw him with Marion he could claim that he had been undercover with a female colleague. At least under the covers would have been true.

"Leave it with me," he said. "I'll see what I can do."

He kissed her on the top of her head before collecting his clothes from the hallway, dressing and leaving.

Dixie spotted him leaving the building and made his way swiftly to his car ready to follow and praying that Jimmy would go straight home, allowing him to relieve his bladder, which felt as if it had grown to the size of a Zeppelin and made wearing a seat belt agony. Fortunately for him Jimmy did drive straight home but at such a leisurely pace that Dixie seriously considered risking losing the car in front and stopping for a pee. As Jimmy drove gently into his driveway, Dixie eased himself and his bladder from his own car and disappeared into a large rhododendron bush and began to pee for Scotland. It took some time for him to empty the entire contents of his bladder, which provided just enough time for the owner of the house, who was tidying his privet hedge at the other side of the garden, to phone the police and for them to show up shortly after Dixie arrived back at his car.

The two uniformed constables were attending what they believed was either a person urinating in public or perhaps the more serious offence of flashing. Either way they were looking forward to an easy arrest and a quick trip back to the station early in their shift. Dixie saw them arrive and swore, annoyed more at having his cover blown than any thought of arrest for relieving himself. He had two options. Pull rank on the two constables and run the risk of them checking his authority to be in their patch or be honest but vague and hope they sympathised with his predicament. On balance he decided that latter option had more chance of working. As the older policeman approached his car, Dixie held his warrant card up to the window which he also opened slightly to allow for what he hoped would be a brief conversation.

"Lanarkshire division. Surveillance duties," he said quietly.

The uniformed officer checked the details on the warrant card before replying, "For fuck sake watch where you're pissing next time. You must have almost pissed on that guy's gardening shoes. You here for much longer?"

"Probably all night mate."

"Lucky you," said the local Bobby who wandered off to placate the resident.

To make it look as if something had happened following the report, Dixie moved his car to a different space outside another house. Ten minutes later the police car drove passed him without any sign of recognition from the officers inside.

"Phew," thought Dixie to himself. "That could have been harder to explain."

A short while after that he was awoken from a brief nap by his mobile.

"Young here," came his boss's voice. "The woman at the address Bell visited has no form or known links with crime. There is a report of a break in there some time ago and Bell filed the initial report. No one was ever done for it, so I suppose he could be updating the victim. What's happening now?"

"Looks like he has turned in for the night. The curtains were drawn earlier and the downstairs lights went off an hour after that. Can I call it a day, Boss?"

There was a long pause at the other end of the line.

"Okay, but be back there by seven tomorrow and take up where you left off."

Dixie groaned inwardly but at least he could go and get a shower and some sleep. He'd need to be up pretty early to get here again by seven but for now he was stood down.

"Thanks, Boss. Good night."

Chapter Twenty Four - Walking on Water

In hindsight, the Water Walkers were a mistake and George knew it as soon as Janine suggested them. But by this stage of the holiday they were relaxing, having fun and he had decided to enter into the spirit of things by being prepared to try anything new. The attendant in charge of the area looked at George suspiciously and asked him to confirm he was below the maximum weight of fifteen stone. Although George was not very tall, he was clearly on the heavy side but he was adamant that he was below the fifteen stone mark so the young lad shrugged and started his usual instructions. He got George to climb the three steps of a platform beside a large inflatable pool of water then climb inside the deflated water-walker. Once George was inside the young lad placed a large nozzle inside the zip section before inflating the sphere. After removing the nozzle and fastening the water-proof flap over the zip, he pushed the whole contraption onto the pool, albeit with difficulty due to the weight inside.

George lost his balance straight away, falling head over heels harmlessly as the sphere rolled out onto the pool. He struggled to his feet several times, only to lose his balance each time and tumble again. Janine was watching and photographing the fun from poolside but was soon laughing so much that it became impossible to take either still photos or any video footage. George could hear her laughing and was a little upset at first but as he realised how happy Janine was he began to ham it up even more, deliberately tumbling and falling for her amusement. If she was happy he realised, the holiday was going well and would surely lead to another spell of peaceful co-habitation. Not necessarily uninterrupted peace in front of the television perhaps, but a pleasant and less lonely existence for him with the accompanying womanly charms of Janine at his side.

As he threw himself around inside the water-walker with increasing energy and force, he failed to notice that the water level was dangerously high, due to the hose used for filling purposes leaking at a section which overhung the pool. Condensation had begun to form around the entire plastic ball and he became oblivious to the higher water level. He found that he could get the sphere to travel in any direction he wished by running like a hamster in the chosen direction then stopping which made the ball surge forward in any chosen direction. He tried this a few times, aiming for the side where he had last spied Janine. As he got to the side of the pool, however, partly due to the extra water from the hose and partly from losing his balance at just the wrong moment, he managed to tip the ball over the edge of the pool. It landed with a thump on the grass beside the platform and then began to roll towards the large boating pond in the centre of the complex. The sphere picked up speed as it ran down the slight hill and would have made it safely to the pond, were it not for a couple sitting on deckchairs sunning themselves on the wide promenade path which surrounded it.

Sharon and Dean had picked a spot for a picnic beside the water but some distance away from the jetty where a stream of noisy children climbed onto or off from the pedalos and kayaks available there for hire. They were enjoying the peace and quiet and were rather sleepy after a lunch of cold foods from the site shop, washed down with a couple of beers. Dean had dozed off with a paper plate of food balanced on his stomach and the plastic knife and fork still in his hands. He was happy to be out of prison; happy to be back with Sharon and happy that he had managed to control his temper on the few occasions which had tried his patience. "Yes," he thought to himself. "Life is good."

Had they had their eyes open they might have seen the large transparent sphere approach them earlier than they did and could have moved out of its way. They might have seen the panic stricken middle-aged figure inside, turning involuntary cartwheels as the water walker ran down the hill towards them. Unfortunately though, with sunglasses on, their heads facing the sun and their eyes closed, they didn't see anything until it was too late.

Dean looked up to see the huge plastic ball heading straight for his girlfriend. He managed to shout her name and she open her eyes in time to see the sphere just before it hit her and flattened the deckchair she was sitting on. Being a strong girl she managed to grab the water-walker and prevent it rolling right over her. Instead it came to rest at an angle, cushioned in her outstretched arms and spread-eagled legs. Inside George found that the sickening motion *had* come to an abrupt stop, which resulted in him falling against the condensation soaked surface mid cartwheel. He then slide slowly down the side of the ball, clearing the mist as he went until his face came to rest staring at the crotch of a familiar fellow guest. He could now plainly read the final word of her tattoo.

"Blyth," it read.

For his part, Dean had watched helplessly as an outsized football flattened Sharon before coming to rest on top of her body and pinning it to the crumpled deckchair underneath. As he watched he could slowly make out the middle aged pervert from the bar slide down inside until his cheek was resting in line with the front of Sharon's bikini bottoms. He watched as the man's face lit up and he was sure he heard a muffled voice say, "You're from Blyth."

Thereafter, Dean's thoughts became shrouded in a familiar red mist as he jumped up and started tearing at the polythene sphere with his plastic cutlery, then his bare hands and finally his teeth to get at the man inside.

Chapter Twenty Five - Jimmy gets a Break

When Chief Inspector James Bell QPM returned home guiltily from shagging his bit on the side he found that his wife, Helen, was in a foul mood and he was initially scared she had discovered his secret. After a few tentative questions he was relieved to find that she was in a rage with her mother as usual, or more accurately with her step-father, who had a drink problem roughly equivalent to his generous pension. He had moved into her family home shortly before she moved out to go to university, leaving her mother to discover that apart from a professional obsession with golf his only other pastime was drinking large quantities of malt whisky, often at expensive golf dinners.

Their marriage had been one born of mutual fear of growing old alone, and so they were at pains to try and make it work, or at least make it seem to work in the eyes of their four children. Helen had seen early on that it was not a happy union and soon stayed at her series of student flats instead of returning home, even for the Christmas holidays. Thereafter she had fielded regular calls from her mother who had chosen her older daughter as confidant for all the neglect and hardship her comfortable middle class life represented.

Missed birthdays, anniversaries, failing to cancel the milk before holidays - all took on immense importance and were relayed to Helen in great detail, much to Jimmy's annoyance as he had to suffer the details second hand after each phone call. Over the years Helen had had to rush off at short notice to assist her mother overcome the latest crisis and for once Jimmy was rather pleased to learn his wife was again about to do just that and intended to take the children with her too.

"It will help take Mum's mind off that dreadful man," she said using the customary endearment she reserved for her step-father on such occasions.

"Oh dear," said Jimmy, managing to hide his delight. "What has he done this time?"

"He has headed off with the golf club on a three night tour of their associate clubs in the North of England without telling Mum."

Jimmy thought for a second, "Without telling her at all?"

"Well, technically without telling her that he was ignoring her insistence not to go, but it comes to the same thing. Will you be all right for a few days? The kids have a long weekend, so I will probably stay till Tuesday. I haven't got anything in for your meals; not that you make it back for many these days, but I like to have some of those healthy options in the freezer when I'm away."

"I'll be fine," said Jimmy reassuringly, as he thought of four days of carry-out meals.

"No chocolate biscuits now. I don't want you to misbehave while I'm away."

At the mention of chocolate biscuits and misbehaving in the same breath, Jimmy suddenly remembered Marion's suggestion of a weekend away at her parents' caravan. It was short notice, but she had said 'anytime he could manage to get away'. This could be the best chance for months and it was being handed to him on a plate, courtesy of his mother-in-law. He had never liked her much but at that exact moment he could have kissed her blue rinsed head.

"Would I misbehave, sweetheart?" he said with a smile.

"Oh I know what you're like at the sight of a packet of Tunnock's caramel wafers. You just don't know when to stop. You are a dear," she added, kissing him on the cheek. "I'll leave first thing in the morning."

With that Helen disappeared towards their bedroom to commence her extended night-time routine.

Before joining her upstairs and hoping she would be sound asleep, Jimmy sent a text, organising something far more sinful and less fattening than chocolate biscuits.

Chapter Twenty Six - Jimmy and Marion

Jimmy awoke the following morning to a very welcome text from Marion saying she was game for a weekend away if he was, which he certainly was. There was a nagging doubt at the back of his mind that somebody might just recognise him, but it was a chance he was more than willing to take.

His wife Helen had risen early, leaving him to sleep on, aware that long lies were something of a luxury to her husband in his line of work. She fed and organised their two children with military precision and was pleased to see Jimmy appear downstairs just before they left. Still in his pyjamas and dressing gown, she had a sudden pang of guilt that the trip to her mother's with the children might ruin his enjoyment of the long weekend they had planned, but when she expressed this concern he reassured her that he would be fine and might even head off somewhere with a colleague who was always suggesting they went fishing together.

She felt better about that. Jimmy and her mother were never comfortable in each other's company, creating a difficult atmosphere for anybody else who was there at the time. On balance she would be much better on her own with the children, especially if her overworked husband could get away from the office for a while. He had not been fishing since they had married but he had mentioned his youthful fishing trips wistfully a few times, particularly when he was distracted by a difficult case, and recently he had been more distant than usual.

He never discussed the details of his work but she had noticed the pressure rise and fall as Jimmy took on a case and it ran its course to a usually successful resolution. She knew he was good at his job, by virtue of his fairly rapid recent promotion, although, being honest about it, she didn't fully understand how he managed it. He was a solid old fashioned copper but was never likely to appear in the final of Mastermind anytime soon. She chased the thought from her mind as disloyal and kissed him on the cheek as she herded the children towards the people carrier which she had already loaded before breakfast with enough clothes and provisions for the three of them to start a new life abroad rather than simply to spend three or four nights at her mother's house.

"You enjoy your fishing trip, dear. I think that's a splendid idea. I hope you catch something spectacular."

"I hope I don't catch anything at all," Jimmy thought to himself with a chuckle and waved his family off before rushing upstairs to shower and pack.

Somewhere across town, Marion Donnelly was relaxing in a hot, perfumed bath which she had prepared earlier and then topped up several times to enjoy the moment as long as she could. On her bed lay a selection of the sexiest clothes she owned, some suitable for public view and many others which were most definitely not. She had never liked being single even after the initial shock of her relatively young husband running off unexpectedly with her friend. She missed him, it was true, but she missed male company in general even more.

After a short period of loneliness, she had taken to online dating to fill the void in her life, only to discover that most of the single men on the sites were either single for good reason or were not single at all. After a series of one night stands, awkward dinner dates and embarrassing silences after meeting up, she had had the good luck to be burgled on one of the days Jimmy Bell had chosen to accompany one of his subordinates on routine duties. The young detective who had been sent to investigate the crime was a mere child in her eyes, clearly deeply in love with his young wife but Jimmy had the tall authority and solidity which most of her recent dates lacked. When his young colleague left, she was determined that Jimmy would take down more than just a list of what had been stolen.

Chapter Twenty Seven - Mother in Law

Helen Bell's mother recovered her spirits quickly with the arrival of her daughter and grand-children. With a mouthed, "I'll tell you all about it later," she focused her attention on the whims of her younger guests. This gave Helen some time on her hands; time she used, as she often found herself doing these days, to reflect on her husband and the state of their marriage.

Had anybody asked her she would have said that they were happily married. Not deliriously as newly-weds are, nor was their sex-life as active as it had once been. Helen accepted that this was one of the inevitable outcomes of her husband's job. He worked very long and often irregular hours. When he came home he was often visibly shattered and she put a lot of effort into providing a peaceful sanctuary for him to relax in. Despite his hard work he would always try and take on his fair share of taxiing of kids and once a month they would all go out as a family for a film or bowling trip followed by a meal together. Jimmy could be lost in his own thoughts on these occasions but he was there and tried his best to pay attention to the children, even in the midst of solving difficult cases. He ring-fenced these outings and their daughter's dancing class as almost sacred duties which allowed her to stick to a regular spinning class at the local private gym. She had kept her figure well through exercise and sensible eating habits and hoped her husband still found her attractive. Their love-making was rare, dutiful and unimaginative but still took place and she put this down at least in part to her efforts to stay young and slim.

The only time she could remember him actively paying attention to a member of the opposite sex had been one Christmas, early in the marriage. They were at her parent's house for Christmas dinner, as was her younger sister, who had been about to finish teacher training at the time. Her sister had been slightly drunk and was flirting with Jimmy who seemed to be enjoying the attention. After the meal, Jimmy had offered to wash up, still at the stage of trying to impress his parents-in-law. Helen's sister Julie had volunteered to help just a little bit too quickly and the two stayed in the kitchen together after everyone had cleared away the dishes with the sound of giggling and laughter wafting through to the living room.

After 20 minutes or so Helen had begun to wonder what was taking them so long and had walked through. As she arrived she saw Jimmy moving back from his sister as if some form of contact had taken place. The door had been closed till she opened it which would have provided a split second of warning, allowing any clinch to be released just in time. Later she had questioned Jimmy about it and he had denied any untoward activity, saying only that he had had to move about to dry dishes and she must have imagined something from any movement as she arrived. Eventually she had put the incident, if incident it had been, from her mind, but had made sure she washed up with Jimmy from then on whenever the family got together for a meal and also that Julie never again had the opportunity to be alone with him.

Jimmy had few hobbies that she could list. He reluctantly fought with the garden to keep it under control when he could although his income, especially with all that overtime, easily allowed Helen to pay a semi-retired gardener to repair any damage Jimmy left behind. Jimmy drank moderately at home and was never drunk in front of the children. He never hit her or belittled her and even occasionally showed affection without too much persuasion. As far as anyone else could tell, they lived a very comfortable and seemingly happy life.

All in all she could hardly complain about her husband. Many of her school friends had made far worse choices, and some were on their second marriage or alone after several failed relationships. It was difficult then to put her finger on exactly why she was unhappy and suspicious of him. She felt guilty even thinking that he might ever lie to her or be playing away with a colleague or female victim of crime. There had never been lipstick on a collar or the smell of a strange perfume which didn't rest on her dressing table. He often showered at work after long shifts but largely because she had advised him to early in their marriage, especially after one long spell of surveillance when a stranger's perfume would have been more than welcome. She tried to put any bad thoughts about her husband out of her head. He was a good man and did a very important and difficult job. Serious crimes wouldn't solve themselves. It was her lot to support his efforts and she had no reason whatsoever to doubt the stability of their marriage.

But fishing?

Chapter Twenty Eight - Surveillance

Jimmy Bell had once said to his wife Helen that half the crimes he was landed with could be solved by going onto Facebook, such was the carelessness with which most people posted on their timeline. He had once found a photograph posted on a suspect's page showing him posing in front of a stolen car which Jimmy and his team were in the process of trying to trace. These online postings were not usually admissible as evidence in themselves but once you knew who had committed a crime you could focus most of your attention on gathering evidence to convict them, having discounted any other suspect. This thought had washed over Helen at the time but now that she found herself at her mother's for a few days she thought of his comments and once more was troubled by doubts about her husband. She felt guilty, it was true, but maybe a bit of casual detective work of her own could put her mind at rest.

With this in mind she texted her husband asking how the fishing trip was going, in order to start a conversation which might allay her fears. There was a delay in replying of two hours which she put down to the lack of a signal or the fact that perhaps he was wading in a river and had left his phone on the bank for safety.

"A few bites so far," came the reply. "Your mum okay?"

"She's calmed down. Just needed an ear and some moral support. Whereabouts are you?"

"Middle of nowhere. Ayrshire."

Then Jimmy added, "Same thing really."

"Who all's there?" Helen asked, starting to do some fishing of her own.

"Some guys who went through the academy with me. Nobody you know. Catching up if not catching fish."

"Well that didn't help," she thought.

"Okay. Have fun and try to relax. See you Tuesday. Love you."

"Thanks. Love you too x."

The next message she sent tried a different tack.

"I've posted pics on Facebook of our two having fun in Mum's garden. Have a look if you get the chance. I'm sure they're really missing you."

Again she felt guilty about what she was doing and even more so about using their own children as bait. Jimmy had a Facebook account but rarely used it. Helen was hoping if he did log on she would be able to see where he was. He was tech-savvy enough to use computers as needed at work but he never seemed to be very clued up at home. The kids had to keep him right most of the time when he tried to do anything ambitious like use Skype. After another infuriating delay came a reply.

"Careful what you post on FB. I'll look later though. Remind them about me from time to time. I got my hands on a beauty earlier. Have fun."

Helen kept her lap-top beside her as her mother went through her step-father's latest crimes and misdemeanours, much to her mother's annoyance. When Helen placed it beside her at the dinner table she felt enough was enough.

"Don't put that there, Helen. It sets a bad example for the children. They'll be wanting their own things at the table next, playing Mario while their dinner goes cold. I wish they had never been invented sometimes."

"Sorry Mum," said Helen as if she were still a schoolgirl and she placed the laptop, still open where she could see it on the sideboard.

Half way through dessert, which was Granny's special rhubarb crumble with cold, tinned custard, Helen noticed that Jimmy had signed into Facebook and had read her personal message with the photos of their children attached. She quickly stood up and logged onto his page. As she had hoped, he had not disabled the location feature and she found herself disappointed to see that he was in fact in Ayrshire. It looked as though he was at a caravan site, which was unlikely, although if he had been added to the trip at the last moment by friends he would have been unable to suggest a better and more comfortable venue. Maybe all was well, she thought, as she returned to mount another assault on the crumble mix. Builders would have killed for the recipe and could have used it to create the world's most solid foundations

Jimmy had once said and now Helen giggled out loud at the thought.

As she helped clear the plates away she started to wonder what kind of fishing was available in the area of the caravan site. Perhaps she could stay up after her mother went to bed at the usual early hour and do some research. Just so she could sound knowledgeable when she next spoke to Jimmy. No other reason.

Chapter Twenty Nine - Old Jock's Big Mouth

After a day or two lying low, Spider began to tour the areas around George's house in Coatshill. He had to be careful, he knew, as police cars and foot patrols were forever passing the house itself. He watched from a distance on several occasions as officers arrived at the address, rang the doorbell and peered through all the windows. It was a warning to Spider but it also suggested that the police had not yet spoken to George Milne or taken him into hiding for his safety. If that was the case then it could also present an opportunity, but only if Spider could find him first. After a further day of frustration he gave up watch on George's house and decided to take a different tack.

Spider knew that George Milne had been a regular at The Ranch and that Janine had worked there as a barmaid. After all, that is where he was caught off guard by them and battered senseless. Then it was where he had managed to kidnap Janine before George ruined his plans yet again. If they were not staying at George's house and he was going to track them down before the police did it seemed the perfect place to start. Walking through the front door would be a mistake but perhaps he could gather some information by phoning the place first.

A quick Google on his phone brought up the smart new website of the pub under its new owners and he decided to use a public phone box to phone. Stopping in a quiet residential area to use a public phone he looked around for cameras and was pleased to see that there were none. He dialled the number and waited.

"Ranch Public House," answered a chirpy voice.

"Hello," said Spider in as friendly a voice as he could manage. "Is Janine McGovern there please?"

"I'm afraid Janine only works here from time to time. Can I help?"

Spider was prepared though.

"I'm a cousin up from Liverpool and wanted to catch up. I haven't seen her since we were kids but only have a few days."

"I'm sorry but she's not here at the moment," apologised the lady at the other end of the phone before adding, "I think she's on holiday and won't be back for a few days yet. Sorry."

"Oh no," said Spider. "I was really hoping to meet up with her while I was here. I have something my father left for her when he died. I had hoped to drop it off. It would mean a lot if I could."

"Wait a minute," said the voice.

In the background he could hear her asking around to see if anyone knew where Janine and George had gone for their week away.

"So they were together," thought Spider. "Good."

I voice in the background said, "Give me the phone."

As the phone was handed over the woman whispered to the man who took it, "It's Janine's cousin from Liverpool. It's important he sees her while he's here."

Old Jock took the phone and after a quick "Hello," let the stranger on the other end of the phone know that Janine was with George at a caravan site in Ayr called Mulligans, staying on the touring pitches in a friend's caravan. He accepted the grateful thanks of the person at the other end of the line and hung up, feeling he had helped in his usual way. It was only after a minute or two that he began to think that actually he had betrayed a secret which he had been sworn to keep except in an absolute emergency. Perhaps a cousin from Liverpool looking to catch up with her was an emergency after all and he had done what was right. The nagging doubt was there, though, and he decided that he would be less open with the information if anyone asked him again.

This was an unfortunate decision for the two uniformed police officers who entered The Ranch an hour or so later still trying to find Janine and George as a matter of extreme urgency. Unfortunately for them by the time they arrived the barmaid had finished her shift and been replaced by the owner who was   unaware of the earlier phone call. The police had visited before but found the bar largely deserted and temporary staff on duty at the time. They had pencilled in a further visit hoping to catch up with more of the regulars or, if they were really lucky, find George and Janine safely enjoying a pint there.

"Have you seen either George Milne or Janine McGov
recently?" asked the older of the two officers when he
reached the bar.

"Afraid not," said the owner of The Ranch. "I think
they're away for a week's holiday at the moment."

"Any idea where they went?" inquired the younger officer
as his older colleague looked round the bar, perhaps half
expecting to see Steven 'Spider' Webb lurking in one of
the corner booths.

"Sorry no. I think it was a surprise, last-minute thing and
they kept it all a bit quiet in case anybody here played a
prank on them or something like that."

The owner looked round at Jock, sitting quietly on his
usual bar stool. Jock had a strangely guilty look on his
face but was taking no part in the conversation taking
place at the other end of the bar.

"Any idea where George and Janine are off to this week,
Jock?" the owner inquired.

Jock looked round in feigned innocence at the three men,
still feeling very guilty at giving away the information so
easily during the recent phone call.

"No idea. How would I know?" he said as if his integrity
had been called into question.

"Just asking, Jock," said the owner with a shrug to the
police officers suggesting that people with thin skins was
a regular feature of his line of work.

The younger officer pulled out a photograph of Spider Webb.

"Have you seen this guy around today at all?"

The owner looked carefully at it as if he was running through a list all of the dodgy-looking clientele of his bar, scoring each one off it in turn which, to an extent, he was.

"He looks a right charmer," he said after a moment. "No, never seen him in here. What about you, Jock?"

"I told you, no," said Jock without even looking at the picture.

"It would help if you actually looked at the photo," said the younger officer.

Jock shuffled off his bar-stool still wrestling with his conscience. He looked at the photo. It looked vaguely familiar but he couldn't put a name to the face.

"Don't know him. He doesn't play darts anyway."

The police officers gave up and one did the rounds of the few other customers in the bar while the other checked the toilets, as if doubting the statements from the locals. He didn't trust anyone in pubs. There was always a chance they were hiding something out of a misplaced sense of loyalty to other regulars or fear of the local hardman. The toilets were empty and after making use of the facilities himself he rejoined his younger colleague in the public bar.

"Nothing," the younger officer confirmed. "Anything in the toilets?"

"Not even hand towels," replied his older colleague and they left with a final request to the owner to let them know if he saw George, Spider or Janine.

Once the police officers had left The Ranch Jock found himself in something of a dilemma. He knew he had promised not to tell anyone where George and Janine were going except in a severe emergency. He also knew that he had betrayed their confidence once and kept it on another occasion; he just wasn't sure he had got it the right way round. One mistake and one success cancelled each other out, he argued, so as far as he was concerned he was even. There was however a nagging doubt regarding Janine's visiting cousin from Liverpool. The accent had been unmistakable, so at least he was from where he said he was. So far so good, but there was something setting off alarm bells deep within Jock's brain and he couldn't quite place it.

Rather than stay at The Ranch until he had resolved matters he headed home for a bite to eat and perhaps a nap to seek inspiration. It was his day off and as usual he was spending it alternating between his home and his local, meeting up with his wife who was a carer for the local authorities between her visits to regular clients. Jock's wife helped people who were housebound with their basic personal requirements such as dressing, washing and feeding, which meant she was away early in the morning and at most meal times on the days she worked. As a result, she and Jock would often meet for a bite to eat mid-morning and mid-afternoon if he wasn't at work, thus spending quality time together with something specific to do to help pass the time.

Jock was quieter than usual, she noted with relief and that had an almost silent lunch of cold meat and coleslaw together around three o'clock. A couple of times Jock looked as if he was going to ask an important question but each time seemed to think better of it and the silence continued.

"Are you heading back to The Ranch later?" she asked.

"Suppose so," Jock answered still lost in his own thoughts.

Not sure what kind of thoughts Jock was capable of his wife decided to play safe and not to pry.

"I might meet you there after work then. I'll be finished around six. You can buy me a drink if you like."

"Aye, that would be good," said Jock without either enthusiasm or proof of having heard what she had said.

"I'll be off then," said his wife and headed back to work. Her first client was eighty and had advanced dementia so she was looking forward to better conversation than she had had with her husband.

Jock dutifully washed the dishes for them both as *he* did whenever his wife was working, and shuffled back to The Ranch still a deeply troubled man.

When he got there he ordered a pint of beer which would usually last him for two hours and returned to consider the problem weighing heavily on his mind.

"Where did they say that escaped bloke was from, Bob," he asked the owner.

"Carstairs I think, so he must be really dangerous," Bob replied abstractly, paying more attention to the horse racing results on the television above the bar.

"I know that, he's a nut job, obviously but where did he come from originally?" continued Jock.

"Barlinnie probably," said Bob annoyed that his concentration was being ruined as the results came in from two races he had an accumulator bet on.

"No," said Jock. "He didn't come from round here and he wasn't from Glasgow so he must have moved here from far away."

"You mean Edinburgh?" said Bob.

"No, far away. He was arrested here, you know, when Janine and George beat him up. You remember!"

"I heard about it Jock but it was before my time. I don't remember the details now but he wasn't from Edinburgh."

"I didn't say he was. He was from somewhere overseas, England or somewhere."

Bob shrugged as much at Jock as the poor performances of both his chosen horses and retreated to wash and dry glasses in the kitchen, something he often did to avoid conversation with Jock.

The racing coverage was interrupted by a short national news bulletin followed by a local news report and the weather. Jock didn't usually watch either but was too deeply lost in thought to use the opportunity to go to the toilet. The national news covered the British Prime

Minister's latest trip to Europe to sort out Brexit and the local report covered the Scottish First Minister's attempts to spoil her efforts. Jock was about to go for a pee when a picture of the man the police officers had been looking for appeared on the screen. Jock reached for the remote control and turned the volume up in time to hear the second half of the report.

"Police describe Webb as extremely dangerous and say he should not be approached by the public," the newsreader said. "He is described as five foot ten in height, heavy build and speaks with a Liverpool accent. If anybody sees him they should contact Inspector Young of Lanarkshire CID on this number."

"Liverpool," thought Jock to himself. "That's a bit of a coincidence."

Nobody had ever said Jock was too sharp for his own good. He very often arrived at the same conclusions as other people, but on average it always took much longer.

"Oh Shit," he said out loud.

"What's up Jock?" asked Bob who had just reappeared from the kitchen.

"I might have fucked things up again," said Jock.

"How come?" asked Bob, not really interested, but intrigued by Jock's honesty and also concerned by his pale complexion.

Jock gave Bob a quick rundown of how he had maybe, just maybe, put George and Janine's lives at risk. Bob confirmed that he almost certainly had and grabbed his mobile phone, dialling the number which Jock had conveniently written down for him as quickly as he could.

Inspector Janice Young was waiting for calls after the news reports of Spider's escape and the public broadcast of his photograph, but was prepared for most of them to be weeded out by her team and any leads to be vague at first. She wasn't prepared though, for somebody who knew Spider's history from firsthand knowledge and George and Janine as friends to phone her and tell her exactly where they were and confirm that Spider had also been told where they were a few hours earlier by the same person. That meant he could be on his way there, or could have already arrived and killed them or any one of hundreds of other possibilities, all bad.

She told the caller to stay on the line and transferred the call to one of the reliable members of her team to get all the details they could, and immediately put a call through to the main police station nearest to Mulligan's, which was in Ayr.

Chapter Thirty - Karaoke

When the holiday had been in the planning stages, George had read on the caravan site's website that there was a Karaoke every Friday night in the main bar, and although he knew the limitations of his star qualities he thought it might impress Janine if he got up and sang. It would certainly surprise her and indeed anybody else who knew him, but he often sang to himself in the bath and in the car and believed that if he practised one of the songs he knew he might become good enough to perform publicly with confidence. The idea had grown in his mind to the point where he was sure Janine would remember the holiday all the more as a result of his performance. After all, Janine loved any reality show on TV where members of the public got the chance to sing in front of an audience and industry professionals. He had noticed her shed a tear or two as the competition warmed up and some of the contestants were voted out of the show. She also loved Tom Jones and never missed the programme where he appeared. Often he found that she could be quite excited after the show or if Tom appeared singing on any other show. So he had practised whenever he could if she was definitely away and swore Evelyn to secrecy even though she had little idea what the constant singing was for.

Early on in the planning stages he made the bold decision to try a Tom Jones number. This was partly due to the fact that Janine was such a fan and had all of Tom's greatest albums in the house, but it was also because he felt he could get more of the notes in Tom Jones' songs than most others that he listened to. His favourite and the one he became most proficient with was 'Delilah'. It had the advantage of fairly few words, a relatively straightforward tune and a chorus he felt sure any audience would join in with. He had grown more confident as the holiday approached and, though still slightly nervous at the prospect of singing in front of a lot of people, he also felt an excitement too.

On the night of the Karaoke, George had to persuade Janine to go along. She had spent some time at the hairdresser's during the afternoon and had popped into the nearest large town to buy the ingredients for a special meal and would have much preferred a romantic night in. George had other ideas and after giving up on the candles and Chablis for the night *she* found herself being dragged to the main bar to witness drunken caravanners singing Bryan Adams songs all night.

"It will be fun," George had assured her before adding, "I think you are in for a bit of a surprise."

Janine nodded with little enthusiasm, deciding that George must have some kind of ulterior motive for turning down a romantic night of passion with her in the caravan.

She sensed that George was in an unusual state of excitement and was suspicious that it had something to do with the Geordie woman he appeared to be obsessed with. Sure enough, Janine noticed the girl at the bar with her tough-looking boyfriend and found her suspicions heightened by the aggressive look the man gave George as they entered.

George simply smiled back at the couple as if they were old friends and bought drinks for himself and Janine before steering her towards a table uncomfortably close to the stage. The night went downhill from there as far as Janine was concerned when the aging master of ceremonies launched himself towards the middle of the stage to false rapturous applause from the crowd and from the tape deck behind the curtains. He warmed up the crowd with a few jokes before introducing the "highlight of the week"; Karaoke Time.   The taped crowd behind the curtain went wild again and many of the audience joined in.

"Let's start with somebody from the bar area," he decided and when nobody stepped forward he picked on a young barman who headed to the stage and gave a reasonable rendition of Wet, Wet, Wet's "Feel it in my Fingers".

Both audiences exploded with cheers and applause at his singing and bravery at being first up, before a massive lady of indeterminate age grabbed the mike before slaughtering "I've got you, babe" which she directed at her inebriated husband who just gave her the fingers at the start of the first chorus.

When she had finished and nobody else immediately volunteered, the MC started bullying a large table of women on a hen night. Eventually one of the older women, who turned out to be the mother of the bride, agreed to get up and stunned everyone in the bar with a flawless version of Adele's "Someone like you". The lack of relevance to a mother and daughter was lost on the crowd as she stepped from the stage to thunderous applause which for once had nothing to do with the tape deck behind the scenes and bundled her daughter into her arms, both in floods of tears.

"Encore," came the chant from table after table till eventually she humbly agreed and returned to the stage. Her encore was Lulu's "Shout", for no particular reason, but *it* was equally good and had her daughter and the entire hen party in tears once more.

George was now quite worried. He had not prepared a second song for an encore. If he got the same response, which he felt was just possible, he would have to sing "Delilah" again. Surely nobody would mind. After all, it was a classic.

By now Janine was fuming. George had paid attention to everything and everyone but her. He must have dragged her here in order to ogle the strangely fit woman from Newcastle again. He kept talking about her, her tattoo and tattoos in general. There was no other reason she could think of. The drinks were extortionate, the venue uncomfortably hot and the whole spectacle of the Karaoke dreadful with the possible exception of the mother of the bride. It wasn't as if either of them liked Karaoke or had ever got up to sing...

"I'll sing," came a strangely familiar voice from nearby which roused her from her thoughts. She looked round to see George heading for the stage.

"Surely not," she thought to herself. "He's just finished his first pint."

But as she stared in disbelief, George Milne walked calmly to the stage with a brief confident smile back at her.

Just as he reached the MC however, a fanfare sounded and the crowd went wild.

"What now?" thought George, assuming there would be some delay to his moment of triumph.

"Well now," said the MC. "We all know what that sound means, don't we?"

George didn't.

The crowd were still cheering, which he began to think was a bad sign as he hadn't started singing yet.

"It's Kamikaze Karaoke Time!" shouted Big Mike the Mic Henderson. "We get to choose the song you sing… (What's your name, mate?)"

George had a feeling things were not going to turn out the way he had planned. He only really knew one song well and the chances of it being the one chosen for him to sing appeared to be quite slim.

"George," he stammered.

"Right, George, let's spin the wheel and see what you are going to sing for us tonight."

Big Mike's assistant, who varied from night to night, depending who was free, wheeled a wheel of fortune from behind the curtain to cheers from everyone in the bar. George felt ill but tried desperately to find "Delilah" on the wheel. As the wheel slowed down he read the songs, his head turning involuntarily as he did so. It wasn't there. As he searched the wheel his spirits plummeted still further. The wheel contained no Tom Jones songs whatsoever. In fact, George didn't recognise any of the songs.

Big Mike spun the wheel while Jim from the change booth at the slot machines, his assistant for the night, watched on with an evil looking grin of anticipation.

At first the wheel moved too quickly to make out the song titles but it began to slow until it eventually stopped at "I'm a Barbie Girl" by Aqua. George felt faint and tried to smile. The crowd laughed as Big Mike pronounced the death sentence and called for silence as the first verse and chorus were played just in case George didn't know the song. It might as well have been The Band of the Grenadier Guards playing Chumba-Wumba for all George cared. His moment of triumph had turned to one of ritual humiliation as he mumbled the words of the song from the screen and returned dejected to his seat. He saw a sea of laughing faces as he went, including the Geordie couple who had taken such a dislike to him. Even the bride had stopped sobbing in her mother's arms in order

145

to laugh at him. Apart from himself the only other person in the bar who wasn't laughing was Janine.

"What the hell were you thinking about?" she shouted at him over the laughter and jeering.

"I wanted to get an encore," George mumbled.

"Are you stupid? You wanted to come here instead of a romantic meal in the caravan with me," Janine shouted over the din. "I wonder why I ever thought of coming back to you."

"I didn't know the words or the tune to Barbie Girl. I was planning to be Tom Jones."

"You would have more chance of being Grace Jones. I have never been so embarrassed in my life."

"You were embarrassed? How do you think I felt," said George. "I was thinking of you."

"If you think for a second I am some sort of Barbie Girl you are more stupid than I thought, which is saying something."

With that she stormed out of the bar to a further cheer from the crowd, with George shuffling behind her.

As he got to the door he heard Big Mike introduce the next performer.

"Right Dougie what are you going to sing for us tonight?"

Dougie Henderson had once been Lanarkshire's best Hot-tub salesman till one too many customer complaints of sexual harassment stopped his meteoric rise towards the

top spot in Scotland. Now he stacked shelves at night in
Tesco but still spent his weekends with his ever
supportive wife Doris at their Ayrshire caravan. He was
no singer but when he took the microphone and belted
out their special tune it still worked its magic on Doris,
providing she had had enough Martini fortified with gin
from her handbag.

As George trudged after Janine towards the caravan,
hoping he would find the door unlocked when he got
there, Dougie fired up the crowd with a murderously
inaccurate version of "Delilah".

"I saw the light on the night..."

George closed his eyes in genuine pain. He could have
sung that so much better, but still the crowd went wild for
Dougie. The last words he heard before the noise died
into the distance were, "Why, Why, Why?"

"Why indeed?" he thought to himself.

Janine had faded into the distance, heading to their pitch
at a speed which suggested an uncomfortable night on the
couch if he was lucky enough to be allowed in and a
freezing night in the car if he gauged her mood
accurately.

"Why Dougie? Why not George? I could have been a
contender. Not just some Barbie Girl bum. Life could be
so unfair."

Chapter Thirty One - Supper of Hot Tongue and Cold Shoulder

George's fears were confirmed when he returned to the caravan and found that the door was firmly locked on him. He tried the car door and found that it too was locked tight. That left the awning of the caravan which he knew was worn and draughty and contained no form of bedding. It was going to be a long and uncomfortable night. He swithered about going back to the bar and having enough beers to block the cold long enough to get to sleep but decided on balance that returning to the scene of his recent disaster was not on. He could picture himself trying to sneak into the bar for a few drinks and Big Mike spotting him from the stage. He was definitely not in the mood for an encore of Barbie Girl.

Instead he decided to go for a walk round the site and try to figure out the best way to get back into Janine's good books. Probably an honest explanation of his plans for the Karaoke would help, but first of all he would need to be on talking terms with her again. Although it was late and a lot of adults were in the bar at the Karaoke, George was surprised to see dozens of children, some in onesies, still playing on bikes and scooters along the roads and pathways of the camp. It was nice he thought to himself that such a safe environment existed where children could play safely and enjoy the kind of freedoms George and his generation had enjoyed when they were younger.

Spider too, watched the children play on their bikes and scooters from his vantage point in the bushes near the visitors' car park. Bloody kids he thought. If he didn't have more important business in hand he would have scared the shit out of them and shut them up. Still, somewhere in this caravan site was George fucking Milne and his bitch of a girlfriend who had knocked him out with her high-heels. He reached up and felt the scar on his head where she had hit him in The Ranch Bar in Coatshill and smiled. Today he would get even with them both. Revenge was a dish best served cold and by Christ, standing in the dark amongst the bushes, was he cold.

Chapter Thirty Two - Should I Surprise Daddy?

By the Sunday of her visit, Helen had decided she still wasn't sure if she had grounds to suspect her husband of lying to her or not. She was sure that he was in Ayrshire; that he might be fishing; that he might be with friends from his days at Police College and that he might be relaxing. The alternative was that he was in Ayrshire, wasn't fishing, wasn't with friends from his Police College course and that he was at a caravan site with somebody else. She had no proof of the latter possibility and confirmation of at least some of the former. For no reason she could be sure of she still had doubts and still felt guilty about having them. Her mum was fine now and had spoken to Helen's step-father by phone, forgiving him and putting their spat down to poor communication. Helen was therefore free to depart and suspected it would be better all round if she did before he returned and the original reason for her visit was remembered.

That left her with two options; return home with the children and wait for her husband's return the following day or to pop over to Ayrshire unannounced and check out the truth of his fishing trip. Home was the obvious and easiest route as the children were tiring of both Granny's house and extended exposure to their mother but what if Jimmy was up to something and the kids witnessed it first hand? She still felt guilty over her doubts but similarly they still wouldn't go away. A solution presented itself when her step father arrived home far earlier than expected with a large bunch of flowers and suggested that he take the children bowling with their Gran. This would necessitate a further night's stay but Helen suggested she had things she could be getting on with if she headed off on her own.

Peace had broken out between Gran and Grandpa and the kids knew a trip out with them always involved a pizza dinner and a bag full of coins for the slot machines beside the bowling alley. The children made the decision for all the adults and Helen found herself heading for Ayrshire alone, still feeling guilty, but sure *that* if Jimmy was with old pals from so long ago he might by now be glad of her interruption and an excuse to head off sharp or book into a Bed & Breakfast with his wife for a romantic night without kids. In fact as she drove she resolved to find a suitable B&B near to the caravan site. If all was well she would entice Jimmy away from his angling friends. Anything fishy going on and she could escape to the pre-booked room to decide what to do next without having to drive all the way home to Edinburgh. She drove on much happier. Thanks to her step-father, the children's love for slot machines, bowling and pizza, she now had a plan.

Chapter Thirty Three - B&B

Helen had a vague idea where the caravan site was and
knew that it was close to the town of Girvan on the
Ayrshire coast. She headed off from her mother's house
and onto the motorway network at a steady pace, not
desperately keen to arrive early but not wanting to delay
the surprise visit to her husband too long either. After two
stops for coffee to reconsider what she was doing and a
further two stops for the toilet to cope with the large lattes
she had drunk she eventually arrived at Girvan.

The town had once been the favoured holidaying spot for
many people from Glasgow and Lanarkshire but had
gone through a bad period after foreign package holidays
took over and the sun of Spain and Greece replaced the
rain of the West of Scotland. Admittedly it didn't always
rain but it rained more often there than in Spain or
Greece. In more recent days the town had tried to re-
establish itself as a short stay destination for more mature
groups or couples, with some success. Many of those who
visited nowadays were the adults who had holidayed
there as children and had many fond memories of sand-
castle competitions, family quarrels and the amusement
arcade on rainy days.

Helen had no such memories and didn't know the town at
all. She headed for the sea front and found a few well
presented Bed and Breakfast establishments amongst the

large villas near the beach. One of them was called the Balmoral and had a sign which read "vacancies" on a swinging plaque in the garden.

Helen parked her car in the driveway and carried the bag of clothes she had taken to her mother's with her to the door, wishing she had smarter luggage.

When she rang the doorbell a small neat lady of around 60 answered with a smile and invited her in. Helen explained that she was on a fact-finding trip and needed a double room as her husband might manage to join her.

The lady smiled a smile which suggested she was unconvinced that any man joining her would be the well spoken lady's own husband and led the way to the first floor and a generously proportioned room which looked out towards the sea.

"Is this okay?" the landlady, who introduced herself as Marie, enquired, confident that there was no fault which could be found in the room or indeed any aspect of her immaculate establishment.

"It's perfect," replied Helen.

"The room is £75 for single occupancy... or... £100 for a couple, which includes full Scottish breakfast served from 7.30 till 9.30 in the dining room downstairs."

There was a pause as Helen admired the view and Marie clearly wondered if the price was putting her off. Helen became aware of the awkward pause and quickly confirmed the rates were fine.

"I'm popping out later to meet up with my husband so I might not know till then if he'll manage to get away. Is that okay?"

Marie smiled again as if she understood the kind of arrangement Helen may have with her possible partner for the night and nodded.

"No trouble at all. Do you know what time you will want breakfast in the morning... or will that depend whether your husband makes it or not?"

"Half eight will be fine either way. Thank you."

"I'll leave you to it then," said Marie. "The room key is there on the bed and the ring has a key for the front door if you need in after 10.30. Make yourself at home and just ask if you need anything else. I'll be in the kitchen baking. It's the Rural tonight and I'm doing the food."

With that she smiled and left Helen alone in the room.

Helen slumped onto the bed in a sitting position then fell backwards feeling suddenly tired. Was she doing the right thing? Why did she suspect Jimmy? What would he say if she spoiled a relaxed fishing trip with his friends? Would they slag him off for having an over-possessive wife? What would she say if she found him shacked up with some female colleague?

As she tried to resolve these questions in her mind, sleep overtook her as it often does with parents of young children, released temporarily from their parental duties. She slept deeply for a couple of hours and found herself having strange dreams. She saw Jimmy in the middle of a deep river, fishing happily for salmon with a bright red fly the size of a blackbird. She called to him and he turned in surprise. As he looked towards her a gigantic fish took the bait and pulled at the rod with enormous force. Jimmy turned to look at it and she watched as the fish pulled him under the water. She screamed his name but he was unable to release the rod and kept being pulled under the foaming current. As he turned towards her for the last time she saw the fish transform into a mermaid, who smiled at her then wrapped her arms round Jimmy who smiled and kicked off his waders, disappearing towards his doom with a broad smile on his face. There was something familiar about the mermaid. As the couple sank from view she realised the mermaid was her sister and woke with a start to discover she was still lying fully clothed on the bed of a strange house in Girvan and was now in a cold sweat.

Her sister Julie had recently separated from her husband and was sketchy about the full details of why. It was a long shot to believe that her husband and sister had anything going between them. Her old suspicions had been buried for so long that the dream had been a shock to the system. Jimmy and Julie? No. That was just too bad to contemplate for her, never mind the children.

"Why are Dad and Aunt Julie snogging?"

No, definitely not. No way. Surely?

Whatever the evening ahead had in store for her she realised she would be better facing it after a shower or even a hot bath which sounded better. By the time she had run the bath, washed herself and soaked in it, it was well into the evening. A quick check of the route on her laptop and a momentary lapse of resolve all soaked up more time as did changing what she was going to wear twice. By the time she left the Bed and Breakfast it was already getting dark and she was starting to regret the two hours she had lost to sleep during the afternoon.

"Goodnight," said Marie with a rather knowing look as Helen made for the front door. "See you in the morning at breakfast."

"Goodnight," said Helen, wondering if the owner listened for movement on the stairs and met everyone as they arrived or left the building. Either way she was too focused now to catch the hint of suspicion in Marie's voice and the delay on the word "you" which suggested it could mean breakfast for a one or two occupancy room by morning.

Chapter Thirty Four - A False Alarm

George trudged round the caravan park in no particular direction, trying all the while to forget about his recent humiliation at the hands of Mike the Mic Henderson and his Kamikaze crowd. George had put so much effort into learning the words and tune for his big moment that the sense of injustice was almost overwhelming. Instead of impressing Janine he had embarrassed her to the point that she had locked him out of the caravan. The holiday had been ruined and the original happy optimism they had shared on the journey over was gone for good.

As he walked round a corner near the static caravans he saw what looked like smoke billowing from the window of the third one along. Maybe it was a trick of the electric light but it definitely looked like smoke from where he was standing. As he approached to get a better look a smoke alarm sounded from inside.

George rushed over to the window, grabbing a set of steps from the neighbouring pitch so he could look in the gap.

....
....

Sharon and Dean returned to their caravan after a great night at the Karaoke. The show had been great fun, the bottled beer on special offer and Dean's football team had won a European Cup tie to boot. As if this hadn't been enough, they had even seen that middle aged pervert, now identified to them as George thanks to Mike the Mic, utterly humiliated in front of everyone including his own partner who had fled the show bar in embarrassment.

They had laughed all the way back to their own pitch and once inside had made love on the floor in some form of strange celebration. Afterwards, while Dean sat naked watching the highlights of the football match, Sharon had gone for a shower.

"Remember to close the door, Pet, or the shower will set off the alarm," Dean shouted.

"Don't worry," she replied. "I'll open the window and let the steam out."

"Whatever," replied Dean intent on watching all three of his team's goals.

....
....

George climbed up the set of three steps which he had leant against the side of the caravan, below the frosted glass of the window where the smoke appeared to be escaping from. He lifted up the window to get a better look inside, hoping that he could warn anybody in the caravan in time to save them when he realised the smoke was in fact steam coming from the a very hot shower.

Sharon had just soaped herself all over and was about to take the shower head down from its wall fitting to rinse it off when she saw the window open wider and George's face appear at the gap.

"DEAN ! DEAN ! DEAN !
DEEEEEEEEEEEEEEEEEEEEN!"

Chapter Thirty Five - A Fear of Spiders

Spider made his way round the caravan park slowly, trying unsuccessfully to look innocent whilst generally hiding in the bushes and trees planted throughout the site. He saw couples of all ages and bloody kids everywhere but no sign of George Milne or Janine. He was just edging round one of the permanent static caravans to get a better look at the far side of the touring pitches when he spotted a couple who looked vaguely familiar. Not the girl, he realised but definitely the man. Too tall to be Milne, but there was something both familiar and worrying about the tall man walking hand in hand with a slim 30-something woman. He had an upright, authoritative air about him, like a policeman.

"Shit," thought Spider. "It's that bastard Bell that did me after the car crash."

Spider hid behind the largest tree he could find quickly and panicked as the couple headed straight towards him. Desperate not to be discovered till he had caught up with his prey he looked round at the nearest static caravan, which had a garden round it and leapt the fence. Still Jimmy Bell and his partner headed in his direction and Spider forced the door of the caravan and threw himself into the darkness, cutting his shin badly on a folded deck chair as he went.

"My fucking shin," he said out loud. "My fucking shin," he repeated cursing who ever had placed a deck chair with such a sharp edge in his way. They would suffer if he had the opportunity.

"My fucking shin," he said again but more quietly as he watched Jimmy Bell pass the gate to the caravan and continue on towards the touring pitches.

Chapter Thirty Six - Living on her Nerves

Miss Blackery had continued to live on her nerves long after the traumatic experience of being involved in a road traffic accident. She had had to deal with the discovery that she lived beside Frankie Cook, one of Lanarkshire's most notorious drug dealers. She had then had to deal with his violent death outside her very front door at the hands of business rivals and the murder of Willie McBride in Frankie's flat, across the hallway from her own. While struggling to come to terms with all of that, she had been involved in her first ever road traffic accident on the way to visit her sister and had helped to apprehend the brutal thug who had caused it. She could still see his twisted face on the grass as she hit him with her umbrella. How she had had the courage to do that she didn't now know but his angry expression and the fists with 'HATE' tattooed on both of them haunted her regularly in her dreams.

She had never moved back to her own flat, instead moving in with her sister and eventually selling the flat in Coatshill. With the money for it she and her sister had fulfilled a lifetime ambition. As children they had spent many happy family holidays at Mulligan's caravan site in Ayrshire in the days before people went abroad and hundreds of families went to Scottish coastal towns for their annual breaks. They decided as a diversion from everything they had gone through recently,*and* to try to recapture the happiness of their youth in their final years, they would buy a static caravan and spend as many days as possible there. It would be different, they knew; they were no longer children and the park had grown enormously and been taken over by a multinational company, but the beach was remarkably unspoilt and just walking along it together again made them both feel younger. In time, Miss Blackery managed to sleep properly most nights and was only occasionally disturbed by the evil face of Steven 'Spider' Webb.

They tended to stay at their caravan during the week to avoid the crowds of children who appeared every weekend with parents or grand-parents and made the swimming pool too busy and noisy to be enjoyable, even without your hearing aids. It was one thing to try to recapture the memories of your own childhood holidays, quite another to have to share it with today's children acquiring their own.

Miss Blackery was sound asleep in her home from home at the caravan site one night, having driven there on her own. Her sister planned to join her the following evening after her routine visit for regular treatment to her corns which were a constant source of pain for her and a steady income stream for her chiropodist. Miss Blackery had walked on the beach and later, finding it slightly chilly outdoors had headed for the swimming pool for a few lengths followed by a good soak in the hot tub. After the rare extravagance of a meal for one in the restaurant she had poured herself a small glass of Baileys and milk, watched the ten o'clock news and gone to bed to read, though not before bringing inside her deckchair and leaving it in the corridor of the caravan. Sleep had overtaken her interest in "The Lovely Bones" and she had drifted off into a deep and refreshing sleep.

In her dreams she found herself as a child again, walking bare footed along the beach, hand in hand with her sister whose own bare feet showed no signs of the painful corns to come. They each held a bucket and spade in the hands which weren't joined and were heading for their favourite spot where a tiny stream spread itself thinly across the sand on its journey to the sea. There they had spent many a happy hour building sand castles with moats full of the fresh, always freezing, water from the stream. In this dream the sun *shone* down from a cloudless blue sky and their long-dead parents watched them sipping tea from a thermos flask whilst sitting on a tartan travel rug as the girls enjoyed the half-deserted sands. The two girls stopped at the stream and smiled at each other; they never quarrelled in such dreams and started building yet another fairy castle fit for a princess, or two. As ever, they built it to the side of the stream and once completed, surrounded it with a moat of diverted water. Then they began the most important task of decorating the structure with shells and feathers. A discarded but now bleached clean lolly-pop stick served as a flag pole on the highest tower for the young Miss Blackery and a white seagull's feather performing the same function for her sister, Charlotte.

"My feather's thin," she heard her sister say and didn't understand.

"What was that, Charlie?" she struggled to ask her sister Charlotte in the dream.

"My feather's thin," Charlotte repeated.

"I don't understand. The feathers are all beautiful," she reassured her sister, slowly feeling the unease of waking reluctantly from a lovely dream.

As she woke slowly the voice of her sister changed to deeper tones and the words became distinct and were now spoken in a rather menacing Liverpool accent.

"My fucking shin," said Spider again in pain as he felt blood starting to pour from the fresh cut on his leg where he had caught it on the sharp edge of the folded deck chair.

He looked round at the elderly, waking figure through the door of the master bedroom and was about to seek retribution for his throbbing shin when she screamed at the top of her voice in sheer terror. It was such a loud scream that Spider was sure Jimmy Bell must have heard it and would be arriving shortly to see what the problem was. He ran from the caravan, catching his other ankle on the deck-chair on the way out and fled to the nearest clump of bushes in the opposite direction from Jimmy.

As he gasped for air to catch his breath he looked round at the path beside the greenery and noticed the unmistakable outline of George Milne heading towards one of the touring caravans.

"Gotcha," he whispered to himself, all of a sudden oblivious to the pain in both lower legs.

Chapter Thirty Seven - Murder in the Dark

George made it back to the caravan to find the door was now unlocked. He took this as a positive sign and quietly opened the door and crept in. He went into the tiny toilet compartment and put the shaving light on. It flashed, fizzled and then went out. He tried the main light but it was dead too and he realised that the electricity connection had slipped out again. He shook his head in frustration and headed back out of the caravan and round to the services connections via the large tear in the rear of the awning.

Spider had followed George and seen him go into the awning of the caravan and assumed he was now inside. He had not been able to see him come out again and decided this was his best chance to deal with the couple whose actions had led him to end up in prison. He quickly and silently ran over to the awning and with a brief look round to make sure he wasn't seen, slipped inside. Once in he pulled the knife from his pocket and grabbed the handle of the door.

"'Now for revenge," he thought to himself and leapt inside.

He felt for the light switch and tried to turn it on but nothing happened.

"Is that you, George?" asked Janine.

"No sweetheart, this is your worst nightmare," replied Spider.

Janine's blood froze. There was pure hatred in the voice and it scared her even before she realised who it belonged to.

"Oh my God," she managed to say just as the light came on confirming her fears that Spider Webb had tracked them down and was about to take vengeance on both her and George. She tried to scream but the fear stopped her vocal chords from working properly.

She managed only a strangled, "Help."

From outside George's calm voice replied, "Coming sweetheart."

Spider turned towards the door realising that George had somehow made it outside again. At that moment though, the lights went out again, the caravan door burst open and all hell broke loose. Janine had briefly seen the terrifying figure of Steven 'Spider' Webb, the gangland enforcer she had beaten to the point of hospitalisation with her high-heels after George had knocked him down with The Ranch's credit card reader. After he had escaped from hospital they had managed to get him rearrested following a car crash caused by George, and he was clearly now out for revenge.

She was aware that after the lights went out again the caravan door had opened and somebody was now involved in a violent struggle with Spider in the doorway. She assumed it was George and knew he would be no match for the vicious thug who had re-entered their lives,

George Milne Must Die

clearly fired up for vengeance. She steeled herself and got out of the fold-down double bed she had expected to share with George after giving him a piece of her mind. Instead now she knew she had to come to his aid or they were both going to die at Spider's hands. She felt for one of her high-heels, her apparent weapon of choice, and felt her way along the caravan towards the door, hoping that she could recognise which of the figures was which and land a blow in George's defence. As she got to the door, however, a stray foot lashed out and she was brought down painfully to the floor. She heard the figures wrestle each other out of the caravan and into the awning where the fight continued. She tried to stand up, only to find that she had landed awkwardly, twisting an ankle as she fell and it would no longer support her weight. She heard the fight come to a violent end outside as somebody's head was hit three times in succession with a large blunt instrument. She assumed the worst and imagined her poor George lying there dead, with blood pouring from a series of head wounds, and knew she would be next.

What she didn't know was that George was still trying to fix the faulty electricity connection in front of the caravan and had not been involved in the fight in any way. Instead Dean had been approaching the caravan with the intention of sorting out the noisy pervert who couldn't keep his eyes off Sharon. On the way though he had spotted a dark figure also making his way towards the same caravan. The figure watched from behind a bush as George returned to the caravan. Dean saw the figure check both a gun and a knife from different pockets of his jacket as if getting ready for a battle and then sneak into

George Milne Must Die

the awning a few minutes behind George, having returned
the weapons to his pockets.

"Interesting," thought Dean. "This guy must really wind
people up to make somebody this angry."

He followed the figure to the awning and listened in. He
heard the figure go in and also George fiddling with
something at the service connections outside the front of
the caravan. He was about to confront George about his
behaviour when he heard the woman inside the caravan
let out a strangled call for help and realised that George's
girlfriend was alone inside with a mad knifeman. Much
as he had grown to hate George he had no beef with
Janine and decided he had to come to her aid. He heard
George call that he was coming to her rescue but heard
him continue working on the electricity connection.

"What a joker," thought Dean. "His girlfriend is in real
danger and he doesn't come to her rescue. I'll speak to
him about that later too, but if he won't help her then I
will. After all, it is the perfect excuse for a good scrap
and it's been such a long time."

Dean reached the door and saw Spider standing inside
with a knife in his hand just as the lights went out. Dean
launched himself into the caravan, grabbing the hand with
the knife as he did. His other hand landed a meaningful
blow to Spider's jaw and battle commenced. Dean was
surprised at the strength of his opponent and the lack of
initial effect of the blows he was inflicting. For his part
Spider assumed in the dark he was fighting George Milne
and was even more impressed at his strength and fighting
abilities. Spider landed a few blows which would have

knocked most people out, or at least slowed them down, but they seemed to have no effect on George. The two men wrestled in the doorway and Spider lashed a kick in the direction he thought George had landed. Instead he caught Janine and heard her fall heavily nearby. He was about to follow up the blow on Janine when a crushing punch to the side of his head reminded him of the business in hand.

"Milne must have been getting karate lessons," thought Spider. He hadn't been hit that hard for years. He launched himself forward and his head connected with the side of Dean's. Both men gasped in pain and they fell out of the caravan and onto the ground sheet of the awning where the fight continued with increased intensity. Dean was starting to worry about the lack of effect of his punches, knowing that his assailant almost certainly still had a gun in his pocket. As they tumbled around the canvas sheet he felt a large wooden mallet and grabbed hold of it. The first blow to Spider's head was inconclusive but slowed him sufficiently for Dean to take aim and land two further blows which stopped all further movement. The fight was over. The lights came on briefly but just long enough for Dean to see the prone figure of Spider Webb on the ground in front of him.

"Shit, I've killed him," thought Dean before dropping the mallet and heading back to his own caravan at speed.

George had heard some of the struggle inside the awning but had somehow put it down to Janine impatiently coming out to see how he was getting on and stumbling over the contents of the awning in the dark.

171

"Why can't she just wait till I get the lights sorted?" he mumbled.

"There we are," he said out loud as the lights came on again and he headed back to the tear in the awning. Unfortunately just as he got there the lights failed again and he decided to give up and just make his way to bed in the dark. As he entered the awning he tripped over something which hadn't been there before, the prone body of Spider Webb and fell heavily, banging his head on a large wooden mallet as he fell. The force cut his head and stunned him momentarily. He felt a trickle of blood on his forehead and slowly realised that he was lying on a body which was, itself, covered in blood. As he struggled slowly to his feet he grasped the mallet in order to put it somewhere safer and as he stood there with the mallet in his hand, looking down at Spider, two large police officers rushed in through the main doorway of the awning, truncheons in hand and *shone* their torches at George. Inexplicably the lights in the caravan came on at the same time and this time stayed on. The door of the caravan opened and Janine peeked out, a high heel brandished above her head in her right hand. She saw George, covered in blood with a mallet in his hand and Spider Webb lying prone at his feet. She rushed to his side and gave him a massive hug. She was almost overcome with relief, tinged with surprise at the outcome of the fight.

"You did it," Janine sobbed.

George looked at the lights and said, "I told you I would sort it."

The police officers looked from George to Spider, at each other and at Janine in her baby doll nightie for a few minutes before either of them could speak.

"Fuck sake," said the older of the two. "Looks like you were ready for Spider without our help. Well done. That is unless you've killed the bastard in which case the paperwork is going to get really messy."

As if to put his mind at rest, Spider gave a faint moan, suggesting his demise had been exaggerated again, and the others breathed a sigh of relief. Janine was now sobbing openly and hugging George as if she was afraid he would disappear.

"You are amazing. You are amazing," she kept repeating in his ear.

George was about to try and explain that he had had nothing to do with Spider's recent wounds when he felt Janine's hand curve round his bottom and squeeze it gently. At that he changed his mind and said nothing.

Chapter Thirty Eight - Dean and Sharon go Home

Dean made his way back to the caravan where Sharon was waiting for him, calmer now and hoping that Dean would be able to remain likewise. When he arrived back covered in blood and with a black eye and swollen mouth she feared the worst.

"What did you do to him?" she demanded the moment he appeared.

"It's okay," he replied "I fought someone else instead."

"How's that okay?" she shouted at him. "You just beat up somebody at random so you would feel better then?"

"Don't be stupid," said Dean. "He must have upset somebody else even more than us, only this guy was going to kill him and his *Missus*. All I did was stop him. He had a knife and fought like a madman so I might have killed him. But only might have."

Sharon looked at Dean and was about to say something else but stopped.

"We better leg it then, before the cops start asking around for who has   a record for violent assault. Remember you're still on parole."

"It had crossed my mind," replied Dean as they both began to pack their bags, then the car, before heading out the camp site in the direction of Newcastle. Any thoughts of arguing over what had happened had disappeared as they reverted back to the well practised routine of fleeing trouble together even to the extent of laughing about what had happened as they put miles between themselves and the caravan site.

Chapter Thirty Nine - Janice's Fears Confirmed

Janice Young was in her car and speeding towards the caravan site in Ayr, prepared for the worst. She knew that both Spider and George Milne were on the site and that Spider was bent on revenge. Janine McGovern was also there with Milne and the two were no doubt up to no good, or were perhaps hiding from Webb. If they met up before the local uniform guys could stop them, she was sure there would be a violent confrontation, with the strong possibility of one or more of the people present being killed. If George Milne and McGovern were innocent they would be toast when Spider found them, but if her suspicions were right and they too were hardened criminals, all bets were off.

As she drove as fast as she could, Dixie held on for dear life. He had tried to drive the car but had been outranked for rights to the car keys and now feared for his safety. He could tell his boss was not fully focused on the road ahead and was taking chances he would never have dreamt of.

"Last man standing, Dixie. That'll be the proof positive," she said under her breath as if Dixie had been involved in the internal dialogue in her head.

"Yes Boss," he managed to say before adding, "Watch that fucking bus... I really thought you were going to hit that bus."

He had just closed his eyes when Janice's phone rang. He answered it despite her attempts to grab it while overtaking on a corner.

"Inspector Young's phone," he said. "Yes. Yes. Really? Yes. Okay. We'll be there in two minutes."

"Well," said Janice.

"You can slow down now, Boss. It's all over."

"And?" demanded Janice without slowing down.

"Please slow down," said Dixie. "If you slow down I'll tell you."

Janice glared at him but slowed down enough for him to breathe properly again.

"Uniform have Spider in cuffs in an ambulance heading for Ayr Hospital. He's badly beaten up but none of it appears to be life-threatening."

"What about Milne and McGovern?"

"McGovern has some minor cuts and bruises but has refused any treatment."

"And what about fucking George Milne?" shouted Janice impatient at the drip feed of information.

"Hardly a scratch on him apparently. Uniform found him standing over Spider with a blood stained mallet in his hand as if he'd just been for a stroll."

"I knew it," shouted Janice. "I fucking knew it. Last man standing, Dixie. Didn't I just say that? Last man standing."

Dixie nodded, rather surprised at what had happened, but unable now to argue against his boss's analysis. Spider was one of the most violent thugs ever to operate in Scotland, if his record was only half true, and he had been beaten unconscious by Milne and his girlfriend without them batting an eyelid. Milne was obviously a dark one who had managed to fly under the radar for years, almost certainly aided and abetted by Detective Chief Inspector James Bell QPM. The implications were huge, but if his boss was going to get any glory for apprehending this gang he was going to make sure a share of it landed on his record too.

Chapter Forty - Old Friends Re-united

Jimmy Bell saw the flashing blue light through the half drawn blinds of the caravan and found his professional curiosity aroused. He saw quickly that it was a local police patrol car and, realising *that* Marion had just started showering, slipped his shoes on to go out and investigate, without giving a thought to how he was dressed. It was part curiosity, part realisation that it just might be colleagues in need of assistance, but it was also an ideal opportunity to grab some fresh air between bouts of sexual activity with Marion.

He saw that the patrol car had screeched to a halt beside one of the touring caravans a short distance from Marion's and he hurried over to see if the officers needed help. As he reached the awning of the tourer he heard relatively calm voices inside and thought for a moment he recognised one of them but couldn't quite place it. Without hesitation he pushed aside the flap of a doorway and entered the space inside to find the familiar figure of Spider Webb on the ground, bleeding, and the all too familiar figure of George Milne standing over him with a wooden mallet in his hand.

George looked up as Jimmy entered.

"Sergeant Bell?" he said.

"You again, and it's Chief Inspector Bell now."

The two officers turned round with added interest in events, now aware that a senior colleague had arrived, assuming he was here as part of the ongoing man hunt.

"You know these two gentlemen?" one of them asked.

"Sadly, yes," replied Jimmy.

"We got a call that an escaped prisoner, one Steven Webb, might be somewhere in Mulligan's looking for a George Milne and his partner Janine McGovern with possible malicious intent. Then a subsequent report of a violent dispute at touring pitch number 101. You know which one's which sir?"

Spider groaned again proving that he was still alive.

"That one's Webb," said Jimmy pointing at the prone figure bleeding into the grass. "That's George Milne with the mallet."

Janine was standing in the corner and Jimmy became aware of her for the first time as she said, "And I'm Janine McGovern."

"You all right, Janine?" Jimmy asked, for the first time showing genuine concern for any of the people involved in the incident.

"Yes, thanks. Shaken but not stirred."

The older uniformed officer spoke into his radio to update the control room of events at Mulligan's, all the while keeping a watchful eye on Spider who didn't look like he was going anywhere under his own steam anytime soon.

"Looks like you had the situation under control, Mr Milne," said the younger officer with a tone suggesting both admiration and surprise. Jimmy rolled his eyes but had to admit to himself that he shared the younger officer's surprise

Janine gave George another hug, ignoring the presence of three bemused police officers, one of whom was wearing slippers, track suit bottoms and a Heart of Midlothian football top.

"You saved us again. You really are my hero," said Janine.

George was more bemused than anyone else but simply shrugged as best he could with Janine holding him as tightly as she was.

Two other vehicles pulled up and the awning suddenly became crowded with members of Police Scotland: two further uniformed officers and Inspector Young with her colleague Sergeant Dixie Dixon.

Janice tried to make sense of what she saw as the uniformed officers conferred quietly in the doorway. On the ground was Steven Spider Webb, only slightly conscious and with blood seeping from several cuts located around his person. Standing over him with a wooden mallet in his hand, was George Milne, and wrapped around him was his partner, Janine McGovern. She looked as if she had been in a struggle, but there was only a single cut on Milne's forehead which didn't look at all serious. "Amazing," she thought to herself. What she found more amazing was the calm presence of her former boss, Chief Inspector Jimmy Bell. If she had any previous doubts about her suspicions that Bell and Milne were partners in crime beforehand, they were completely dispelled now. She looked round at Dixie with a knowing look and he returned it with a nod of his head.

"Last man standing," she whispered to him quietly enough that nobody else could hear.

He nodded again.

Janice turned to her former boss and in a very businesslike manner asked, "What are you doing here, Sir?"

Jimmy had been splitting his gaze between all the figures in the tent as well as suggesting to the senior uniformed officer that one of them *should* set up a cordon of tape round the area and *make* sure an ambulance was on its way for Spider, who was now groaning more regularly.

Jimmy turned to Janice with what she recognised as a slightly guilty expression.

"I was... on holiday at the site... when I saw the blue lights. Bit of a coincidence really."

"Bit of a coincidence, right enough," Janice agreed exchanging another knowing look with Dixie.

"Were you first on the scene, then?" Janice asked.

The senior uniformed officer chipped in, "No Ma'am, we got here first, but it was all over by the time we got here. Inspector Bell is it.....?   popped over to see if we needed a hand."

Janice nodded, still wondering what the hell Jimmy was doing here, and in no way convinced of his cover story. The two of them gravitated to a spot outside of the awning to talk.

"I'll just get off, then," Jimmy said to Janice's surprise.

"We'll need a full statement at some stage, Sir," she added as he headed out of the tent flap.

"Sure... of course. I'll keep in touch," came the reply as Jimmy disappeared through the crowd and into the cover of relative darkness.

Janice re-entered the awning and turned to George.

"So what happened, then?"

Before George could say a word Janine answered for him.

"This bastard appeared from nowhere, I thought he was meant to be locked up, and he attacked me inside the caravan. George was outside sorting the lights, which are bloody lethal if you ask me. Anyway I managed to shout for help and he must have heard me and waded in without a thought for his own safety. He really is a tiger when he has to be.   If it hadn't been for George we would have both been dead."

Janice looked at George, still standing with the mallet in his hand. He nodded and smiled in a way that meant, "What she said."

"We'll need statements from you both, but that can wait."

As she thought things through, trying to piece together what had happened here she started to formulate a plan. If Milne and McGovern were here, and were kept here, and Evelyn Cook was still in protective custody then there was nobody minding the shop back in Coatshill. This could be a golden opportunity to do a bit of digging into the private life of Milne and nobody would be any the wiser. She smiled as she decided what to do next.

"Okay, looks like you guys have had a lucky escape. We'll get this thug back under lock and key after he's been patched up. Meanwhile you two have a cuppa and chill. It seems fairly straightforward what happened here, so we can leave your statements for now. Could you remain on the caravan site though for the next few days? No point spoiling your holiday on account of this guy."

George and Janine nodded.

"Of course," said Janine, still hugging George, who found the mallet being removed from his grasp and placed inside a large evidence bag by one of the uniformed officers. "We had planned to stay another two days anyway."

"Excellent," said Janice. "You guys head back into the caravan and try to relax. We'll sort things out here and I'll pop in for a chat in a minute."

George peeked out of the window of the caravan through the curtains and saw the large crowd outside, now shepherded back to a suitable distance by several uniformed police officers. Near the front of the crowd he saw Mike the Mic Henderson looking on. George smiled to himself. Maybe he would get a bit more respect from people on the site after this. Nobody would treat George 'the Mallet' Milne like a Barbie Girl ever again.

When George and Janine had gone back inside the caravan, Janice turned to Dixie.

"Come with me, Dixie. I've got a little job for you to do back in Coatshill." As they made their way outside the tent to a quiet spot she added, "This is the ideal time to search Milne's house. We know he'll be here for a few days now and we will even have uniform here to make sure he does stay. You head back and go through the house like a dose of salts. He must have something incriminating there; drugs, notes, loads of mobiles, even large bundles of cash. You find it."

"Right, boss," said Dixie. "Give me a shout when the warrant's through and I'll get a team together."

Janice looked at him. "Don't be soft, Dixie. Just go and break in. Do it all yourself. We keep this quiet till we find the dirt on Milne then we go public. If he's on bloody holiday with Jimmy Bell then who knows what other friends he has in the police? Get back there now and search his house."

"But it's midnight, Boss," said Dixie buying time. He wasn't keen on Janice's plan.

"Just do it," she snapped back at him.

Janice looked round the dwindling crowd, half expecting to see Jimmy standing watching her. She realised she hadn't even asked which caravan or chalet he was staying in. It didn't much matter though. She had got him red-handed associating with George Milne and once Dixie uncovered evidence of crime from the house she could then move on Bell. Internal investigation would have to get involved then. She watched Dixie drive off in the car.

"Don't let me down, Dixie," she whispered under her breath.

As she gazed thoughtfully into the crowd she noticed a woman standing off to one side who was familiar. At first she wondered if she was a villain of some kind or the wife of somebody she had had dealings with in the past, but the smart, tasteful way the woman was dressed suggested otherwise. It was somebody she had met before though, of that she was certain; but where and who had she been with? Her gut instinct was that it had been somebody dodgy, but the name didn't appear.

Chapter Forty One - Helen Finds Jimmy

Helen started her journey to the caravan site with a steely resolve but she found that the nearer she got the more her doubts returned. In her head it was difficult to prepare for both of the likely possibilities. If Jimmy was indeed enjoying a relaxed fishing trip with old friends then she would need to have a good reason for interrupting it. The excuse of being free from the kids for the evening and deciding on a whim to join him and try to entice him away for a romantic liaison was plausible she felt, but only just based on their usual romantic liaisons. If on the other hand she found him ensconced with another woman she would have to be ready for that too. The second possibility would need to result in an angry but measured response and that would likely spell the end of their marriage or at the very least, the continuance of it on very different terms. She found the requirement to drive on unknown roads while simultaneously being prepared to either entice or berate rather challenging. On balance she decided it would be easier to hope for the best and to assume she would react accordingly to the worst. That approach at least allowed her to focus on the unfamiliar roads.

She arrived at the entrance to the caravan site after less than half an hour's driving and realised for the first time how big an area was covered by the facility. She had no clear idea where Jimmy might be, assuming he was still within the confines of the grounds. A slow tour of the roadways only afforded a glimpse of how many footpaths and other parts of the camp were inaccessible by car. After a second tour round the internal roads she was about to give up when a police car came screeching into the camp with its blue light flashing. A short while later it was followed by another marked car and what was obviously an unmarked police car with more flashing lights. All three cars headed in the same direction, and with no other line of inquiry as to her husband's whereabouts, she followed them at a safe distance.

The first police car had stopped near a touring caravan and had both doors wide open, suggesting they were answering an urgent call. The second had arrived and blocked the far end of the pitch while the unmarked car was pulling up to block the nearest end. Two plain clothes officers were getting out of the car, one female and a younger looking male officer. They made their way into the caravan awning at a determined pace but without running.   Helen was tempted to follow them inside after she had parked her own car in the neighbouring row of touring caravans, but decided on balance it would be foolish, not to mention potentially dangerous.

She watched from inside the car, half expecting a violent struggle to erupt from inside the awning or the caravan itself, but nothing happened for almost 10 minutes. Then an ambulance arrived with its blue lights flashing and made its way through the growing crowd of spectators who had gathered outside and were starting to surround the caravan just as a uniformed officer came out of the awning and ushered them back. He escorted the paramedics into the canvas and returned to send the crowd further back.

Helen felt her stomach tighten. What if Jimmy had been hurt? Maybe the ambulance was there for her husband who was lying dying inside. She had been doubting his faithfulness and there he was bleeding to death doing his dangerous duty secretly so as not to worry her and the children. All manner of thoughts went through her head and she found herself getting out of the car and walking towards the crowd, unsure what she was going to do but determined not to leave the scene before knowing for certain that Jimmy was all right. As she got to the edge of the crowd, the paramedics appeared with a stretcher carrying a man who was clearly not Jimmy. He looked as if he had just lost a title fight to Mike Tyson's big brother and was groaning and swearing audibly. Jimmy rarely swore and never used any of those particular combinations of words.

Perhaps he was still inside and had been killed by this man. She started to push her way through the crowd towards the uniformed officer, with the steely resolve of a wife worried that her husband was in mortal danger. Before she had made it half way through the rows of campers watching the drama unfold she saw Jimmy walked unscathed out of the awning, deep in conversation with the woman who had arrived in the unmarked police car. Their faces were briefly well illuminated by a light from somewhere inside and she recognised the woman as a former colleague of Jimmy's, Janice somebody whom she had once met at a social event when they had all sat at the same table.

"Oh my God," she thought to herself. "Jimmy has been working undercover and all this time I have been suspecting him of having an affair. He's even wearing those dreadful pyjama bottoms and Hearts top I always want to throw out, just to blend in with the people here."

She felt dreadful and turned quickly so that Jimmy would not notice her. She knew he was safe. She knew he was working with colleagues from the police and all of a sudden she knew she shouldn't be there and certainly didn't want him to find see there. Wracked by guilt, she walked back towards her car and after watching her husband walk off into the distance and Janice return to the awning before coming out again and briefing the other detective, she got in *and* switched on the ignition. It was obviously a well planned police operation with her husband in charge; doing what he did best. How could she have doubted him? She found that tears were forming in her eyes and she felt terrible. Still hoping to escape the camp without her presence being discovered by her husband she started driving towards the gate without remembering to put her headlights on. At the gate yet another uniformed officer who had arrived unnoticed to her, with his colleague was controlling traffic. He waved her down and she thought for one moment she might be discovered.

"Pop your lights on, Madam," said the policeman. He waved her out of the camp once she had put them on and she smiled at him, as if to say 'silly me'.

"Silly me, indeed", she thought. "Silly, silly me. A brave husband keeping everyone safe from thugs like that and protecting me and the children from the knowledge of how dangerous his job was. How could she have suspected him?"

She felt the tears flow as she drove and even had to stop once to wipe them away from her eyes in order to see the road.

"Silly, silly me."

She was still wiping tears from her eyes as she arrived back at the Bed and Breakfast and used her key to let herself in, hoping the owner would not be about. She was out of luck. Marie had heard the car on the gravel of her driveway and thought it would be a chance to see how many people would be around for breakfast.

She reached the hallway just in time to see Helen arrive alone and run up the stairs, obviously in tears.

"I guess the date hadn't gone very well," she whispered to herself and jotted down, "Room one, one for breakfast" so that her husband knew how many to set the tables for in the morning before he headed off to work.

....

Back at the caravan site Jimmy went back to the caravan where Marion was waiting for him. Earlier she had come out of the shower to find him gone. In fairness, he had shouted that he was going to see what the blue lights were all about, but she hadn't heard him. She saw flashing blue lights in the distance when she came out of the shower, naked except for the towel wrapped around her head, and correctly figured out that professional curiosity had got the better of him. He was now back safe and sound and they could take up where they had left off.

"I thought you had found something more interesting than me," she said as he came in, sitting still naked on one of the benches at the opposite end of the caravan to the door.

"More interesting than you?" replied Jimmy."Can't think of anything that could be more interesting than you at this exact moment in time. Silly you."

"Silly me, silly, silly me," said Marion as she took the towel off her hair and walked over towards the door where Jimmy was standing. "Silly, naughty little me. I thought the police had arrived to arrest me. But I seem to have slipped through the long arm of the law again. Perhaps you should arrest me instead. I can't expect to evade the law for ever, can I? Go on, officer. Put the cuffs on me. I'll cooperate, honest I will, although I can't promise to come quietly."

Chapter Forty Two - An Unwarranted Intrusion

Dixie was a troubled man as he drove to Coatshill
frowning all the way with a deep sense of unease. Yes, he
and his boss had found George at the caravan site having
beaten one of Britain's hardest villains to within inches of
his life whilst sustaining only a small scratch on the head.
Yes, McGovern was with him and they appeared to be in
hiding together, or had *lured* Steven Webb to a planned
settling of old scores. Yes, they had discovered that Chief
Inspector Jimmy Bell was there too and was therefore
complicit in whatever Milne and McGovern were up to.
Despite all of this he was unhappy to be on his way to
break into a house illegally, even if it was George
Milne's. He was a graduate police officer hoping to scale
the heights as quickly as he could and did not want
anything dodgy in his past career which could reappear in
the future to bring him down. For that reason alone he
was unhappy with the thought of doing anything illegal.
The other major problem he had to contend with was the
fact that he had never broken into a house before and had
no clear idea of how to do it without causing sufficient
damage for the search to be immediately obvious. He had
seen enough houses which had been broken into and was
aware of how it had been done, but now it was his turn to
burgle somebody he wanted to do it properly. There
would be nothing worse than if it did become known later
that he had carried out the search but had made a real

mess of the locks in doing so. That would smack of a total lack of professionalism.

He arrived at the address in the middle of the night, still worrying about how to get in. The street was very quiet and there were no obvious neighbours watching as he pulled up a respectable distance away to have a good look at his first, known in advance, future crime scene.

As he waited there he noticed a local police patrol car spot him sitting there and it slowly pulled up behind him.

"Not again," he said under his breath.

The two uniformed officers were obviously checking out the car to see if it indicated anything suspicious was going on. News of Spider's arrest and the fact that both George Milne and Janine McGovern were now safe obviously hadn't reached them yet and they would still be working on the instructions to keep a close watch on any of George Milne's known haunts, including his own home. Dixie couldn't see who the officers were, but was certain he would probably know at least one of them if they got out and came round to speak to him. The last thing he needed, considering the dubious legality of his current mission, was it being noted in any official or even unofficial way. He watched the figures in the car behind him receive a reply which would obviously be something along the lines of, "It's a bloody police car".

The car indicated that it was pulling out into the road again and as it slowly passed by, Dixie recognised an old sweat from Coatshill Station by the name of Gordon McIntosh in the passenger seat. Dixie discreetly gave him the fingers from the lower part of the driver's door window and Gordon returned it subtly by moving his hand across his mouth with two fingers in Dixie's direction, all without looking round.

The property he was about to break into was one of four flats in a former local authority block. They were sometimes euphemistically called 'Cottage Flats' by estate agents now that they were almost all privately owned. It didn't look as if it had been made any more secure than any of the other flats in the block. It had modern double glazing and a newish front door but this had several glass panels in it and was not the typical massive structure most drug dealers would install to keep their rivals out or delay the forced entry of police raiding squads. It all looked... well... ordinary. It was as unremarkable as George Milne himself seemed on the surface but Dixie quickly reminded himself that this unremarkable man had just beaten the shit out of one of Frankie Cook's most feared former enforcers.

"Proceed cautiously," a voice in his head suggested.

He had realised on the way over that he had no suitable tools in the car with which to force an entry but *he* had stopped at his own house on the way and brought his meagre collection of tools in a new-looking and largely unused plastic tool box. He hoped it would hold sufficient aids to break in, containing as it did one claw hammer, several screwdrivers of differing sizes, a craft knife, some gaffer tape and unopened boxes of nails and screws. He had looked at the contents while loading it and realised it would have made any tradesman or even serial killer laugh out loud at the lack of options which it offered. He took the tool box from the boot as he headed over to the flat which was, mercifully, on the ground floor, still unsure what he was going to do once he reached the door. Fortunately he knew from his days on the beat that the ground floor flats of these properties had a back door as well as a front one and he made his way quickly to the rear and out of sight of the street.

The moment of truth regarding Dixie's housebreaking skills had arrived and he wasn't overly confident he could manage it easily. He tried the door in the vague hope it had been left open but it was locked. It had a single Chubb type lock on it which looked like it had been the original one installed when the houses were first built. That didn't suggest much effort on the part of George Milne to improve security. Only a criminal supremely confident in the knowledge there was nothing incriminating to find would leave their house so badly protected. Dixie examined the lock to see if there was any easy way of removing it from the outside. Not surprisingly, he discovered that there was not. He examined the hinges, the glass panel and the door surround, looking as much for inspiration as a weak point. He had just decided to try and remove the glass panel, with the intention of replacing it somehow in daylight, when his foot caught a small metal casting of a cat which was sitting on the edge of the rear door step. He cursed the slight noise it had made and then realised that it had made a clinking sound as it moved, as if there was something hidden inside it.

"Surely not," he thought to himself.

Carefully lifting it up he discovered a Chubb style key lying underneath the cat.

"What a cool character this Milne bastard is," he thought. "He is almost taunting me to find try and find something. This is going to be a fool's errand or... maybe there is some kind of booby trap inside."

This thought was a worrying one, although rationally, Dixie knew it was more likely that he would find nothing incriminating. He tried the key, and after a bit of a struggle it turned and he was able to open the door. He waited on the threshold, fearing an alarm, or huge but silent killer dog, or even a shotgun tied to the door handle and pointing at his midriff, but nothing happened. He slipped quickly inside and closed the door behind him. He had brought a head-torch to provide enough light for a search without using the house lights and he now put it on. He made a quick survey of the rooms to confirm, if it were needed, that he was alone in the property then he started as thorough a search as he could manage, starting with the master bedroom. He checked every drawer, every cupboard, under and behind every bit of furniture.

He continued the search throughout the house in the same way, including the attic. He even tapped every floorboard in the flat to see if any were loose. Almost every one of them was, but the carpets were glued down and he couldn't find any area of easy access to the boards and the spaces underneath. If this had been a search with a warrant and a large team he would have hauled up both carpets and boards to make sure. But, as he was painfully aware, this was an unauthorised search. Nothing! After an exhausting four hours or so he gave up. He went back to the door he used to enter the flat and gathered his thoughts. The flat had no additional security measure as you might expect if it held anything of value or incriminating material. He had got in using a key that a child could find, even if it had taken him twenty minutes to discover it. He looked out to the shared garden for inspiration. It only confirmed that the residents of both levels of flats hated gardening. At the bottom of the garden, though, was a well kept shed.

"Ah ha," he thought. "If nobody enjoys gardening, and they obviously don't, why would they have such a large shed in such good condition?"

Breaking into the shed presented a similar problem to the one he had faced to break into the house itself but with the added complication that he would have to do it outside with the possibility that one of the neighbouring residents could see him if he made a noise or if they happened to look out of a rear window. As he considered his small selection of tools again he noticed a £20 note lying beside the back door and was briefly tempted to pocket it for all the trouble he was going through, he even got to the point of reaching out to grab it to cover the costs of a good breakfast. He stopped himself and withdrew his hand, but not before seeing a padlock key sitting beside the bank note. It was on a key ring and had a tag attached to it which he managed to read with his head torch. It said "Garden Shed".

Dixie's professional skills as a former crime prevention officer were offended by how easy Milne was making this for him but he wasn't going to look a gift horse in the mouth. He took the key and switched the head torch off. Then as quietly as possible he went out of the back door and walked quickly to the shed. The newish padlock opened without difficulty and he went inside. In cartoons and sit-coms people often stand on garden rakes which spring up and hit them in the head. It makes viewers laugh and they assume it does not happen for real. Any doctor or nurse who works in an Accident and Emergency department will tell you that it is a common injury they have to deal with and it is far from funny for the victim. They might further advise that you should lean a rake against a wall with the prongs at the highest point or at least pointing away to avoid the possibility of somebody standing on them and levering the weapon forward at a deadly speed. George had done neither and Dixie stood on a rake in the darkness and was immediately struck by the handle around his right eye. It hurt and he yelled out involuntarily.

"You bastard," he said louder than he meant to and froze, realising his mistake. He waited, half expecting all the surrounding lights to come on and for somebody to appear with a poker or other weapon to investigate. After five minutes he realised this was not going to happen. The sturdy shed must have muffled his cry sufficiently to leave the local public sleeping soundly in their beds, Dixie assumed.

What Dixie didn't realise was that Bob Brown was continuing his practice of peering out of the window at regular intervals in the hope of catching the weed thief next door, unaware of George and Janine's adventures elsewhere. This included the hours of darkness when he often had to visit the toilet and used such occasions to watch from behind his net curtains to see if anyone was about. He had always been disappointed before but on this night, by chance he had struggled to sleep. Perhaps it was a premonition. As he gazed out of his window he noticed the shed door was open. It had not been open four hours before when he had looked at it previously.

"Got you," he whispered to himself.

He heard a muffled curse and shortly afterwards saw a figure leave the shed, holding his eye. It was too dark to confirm that it was George Milne but Bob decided it could hardly be anyone else. he watched till the figure went into the back door of Milne's house and phoned the police.

"I want to report a theft," Bob began.

The duty sergeant was surprised to receive such a calm call at that time in the early morning but professionally asked for details.

"My next door neighbour is stealing my plants at night. I've just seen him. He also poisons the ones that are left on my side of the fence."

The duty sergeant stopped taking notes for a second.

"Your plants?"

"Yes my plants."

"Are these valuable plants, Mr Brown?"

"They are to me."

The duty sergeant was about to suggest Bob phone back in the morning when he noticed Gordon McIntosh walk into the station with his partner. He loved winding Gordon up and saw a golden opportunity.

"Okay Mr Brown, we'll get a car there as soon as we can. Gordon ! We've got a major theft just witnessed at the top of Coatshill. You two head up there pronto."

Gordon groaned. It had been a long shift and it was almost finished. He was rather hoping for a quiet cuppa before heading home. If there had been a break-in he could be tied up for hours.

"What's been stolen, Bob?"

Bob the desk Sergeant smiled, "I'll give you details on the way. Here's the address."

Gordon took the piece of paper he was handed and looked at it briefly before heading for the door. Then he stopped as he recognised George Milne's address.

"That's okay Sarge," he said. " CID are already all over that place. It must be something really important. Best leave it to them."

With that Gordon headed for the canteen leaving the duty Sergeant bemused at his desk.

....

The pain around Dixie's eye was intense and he could feel it swelling up. He had a good mind to abandon the search and go home to put a cold pack on the affected area. He would get some stick at the station when his colleagues, including Gordon McIntosh no doubt, saw what would surely be a very black eye and he began to wonder what time the local branch of Iceland opened in the morning. He switched his torch on and searched the shed. It was, not surprisingly, full of gardening tools and also contained a far superior collection of tools to his own. None of them looked as if they were used on a regular basis, which went a long way to explaining the state of the common garden area. Nothing in the shed suggested to him that it was used to house anything but tools, some empty plant pots and a lawn mower.

"Of course it doesn't," he suddenly thought. "If it did it would have huge locks on it and there would a dog from the same litter as the Hound of the Baskervilles running loose around it. I wouldn't have found the key for the shed in the kitchen with a label marked 'Garden Bloody Shed' and I wouldn't have found a key to the house under a metal cat to allow me to get in."

The pain in his eye was throbbing and he suddenly felt foolish for being there at all and for doing what Inspector Young had suggested without insisting on a warrant. He felt tired too. It was almost five in the morning and he hadn't slept much recently with all the surveillance he had had to carry out on Jimmy Bell. Suddenly all he wanted to do was go home and sleep in his own bed. He locked up the shed, locked up the house, put his tools quietly back in the boot of his car and went home, having first sent a text to his boss confirming that he had found nothing and would be in late the following day. He switched off his mobile, unplugged the house phone and fell into a deep sleep, dreaming of caravans and childhood holidays.

Janice Young was woken early, after only a few hours sleep, by the sound of a text arriving on her phone. She reached out for her mobile phone still half asleep and knocked it onto the floor beside her bed. Resisting the strong temptation to ignore it and go back to sleep she moved her arm around on the carpet until she located it. Still groggy she pressed the Home button but sprang upright when she realised the text was from Dixie.

"That's my boy," she said opening the text but her face fell as she read it. "Nothing? How the fuck could you find nothing? You obviously weren't searching hard enough."

She used the speed dial to call Dixie's mobile but found his phone was "currently unavailable".   Then she did the same with his home number and got the same result.

"Useless bastard," she screamed. "No wonder your wife left you. It wasn't just because she was a copper's wife and they always do."

The words "copper's wife" echoed in her head as she slowly calmed down. It wasn't Dixie's fault and she knew it. Of course many police officers' marriages fail, it was the nature of the job: the long hours, the unsocial shifts and the internalising of the trauma of what you had to deal with sometimes. It was inevitable really. She could think of very few of her colleagues who were still with their wives, or at least first wife. The longest successful marriage she could think of was Jimmy Bell of all people.

"Oh Shit. Oh Shit," she thought.

Jimmy Bell's wife, Helen. That was who she had seen in the distance at the caravan site. Why hadn't she realised it before? If she was at the site too then maybe Jimmy had simply been on holiday with her and perhaps their kids too.

"Oh Shit. If I've got this all wrong and it is just a coincidence after all then I have ordered Dixie to break into a house with no justification whatsoever. What if Milne isn't a crook but just some unlucky bastard who keeps having shit happen to him?"

She sat on the edge of the bed trying not to think about what would happen to her if Jimmy found out she had had him followed and suspected him of being a bent copper. At least she hadn't mentioned his name to Internal Investigation. Questions swirled around her head: Was there any way Jimmy could find out? Would Dixie's break-in be discovered? Would they be identified as the ones responsible?

Most of all though, she focused on one question. Could she blame it all on Dixie if she had to?

Chapter Forty Three - Breakfast for One

Breakfast was a lonely affair for Helen Bell the following morning. She had struggled to get to sleep after she returned from the caravan site and when she finally did drop off it seemed like no time at all before the alarm on her phone woke her again. She showered and dressed quickly, then realised she was very early for the slot she had booked for breakfast. She thought about going down before the allotted time but was now wary of her hostess, who seemed to be taking far too keen an interest in her guest. In the end, though, she succumbed to the smell of frying bacon, suddenly realising she hadn't eaten during the previous evening and went downstairs 20 minutes early hoping she could have a quick, early meal and leave for the safety of her home.

Marie smiled her knowing smile as Helen came into the dining room to join the other guests, two other couples who appeared normal, married couples spending quality time together. Helen thought again of all her wild doubts about Jimmy and felt the guilt and shame well up in her again. She only just managed to prevent tears forming in her eyes as she asked for coffee and a full Scottish Breakfast. She wasn't sure she would manage to eat all of the fried food on the plate, a meal she would never have considered at home, but she knew she was very hungry and had a long drive ahead.

The television was on discreetly in the corner of the room showing the news. The national news was dominated by political discussions regarding Brexit but after 20 minutes on the subject the presenters handed over to their regional colleagues. The Scottish headlines started with the reassuring report that escaped prisoner Steven Webb was back in custody after having been arrested at a caravan site just outside the Ayrshire town of Girvan.

Helen's attention was immediately drawn to the television and she found herself looking at the usual thick-set crime reporter standing outside Mulligan's Caravan site where, the night before, Steven Webb had been recaptured after a violent struggle. He was again safely behind bars and a uniformed Inspector appeared to reassure the public that the danger which he had posed was now at an end.

"Oh my God," she thought, Jimmy must have been staking out the site, waiting for this guy to appear. Had Jimmy been the one to subdue him to the point of needing a stretcher to make it back behind bars? She hadn't seen Jimmy enter the caravan and he had definitely been in before either the second uniformed pair or the two plainclothes officers arrived. He must have faced the man alone, with only the hope of back-up on its way, and yet he hadn't had a mark on him. How brave he was, and, also, he must be pretty useful in a fight. Her brave, gentle giant. She had never really seen him angry and there had never been even a hint of any hidden propensity for violence. How lucky she was and how stupid she had been to ever doubt him.

The coffee arrived quickly and she poured herself a cup, unusually adding both sugar and milk. She felt faint and didn't want any unnecessary embarrassment before she could leave. As she drank her coffee and waited for the irresistible smells from the kitchen to translate into a delicious breakfast she tried to put the events in some semblance of order. How did she find herself alone in a Bed and Breakfast, in Girvan of all places, while her husband dealt with a brutal thug who was a danger to the public, all the time unaware of his wife's groundless suspicions of infidelity? The tears started to form again as Marie brought a mountainous plate of cooked food through from the kitchen.

Marie obviously noted the tears and misread Helen's mood. She placed the plate on the table and as she started to walk away placed her hand on Helen's shoulder briefly and whispered, "*They're* not worth it, dear."

Helen was a little confused but started into the food, relieved to be finally eating something.

Not worth it? Not worth it? What did this woman know? Jimmy was worth it all right. Worth a thousand ordinary men. She had a good mind to follow her into the kitchen and set her straight but the smell and taste of the bacon and eggs on the plate stopped her for now.

She focused on the food in front of her and only looked up at the other guests when she had brought the feeling of starvation under control. The couple to her left were obviously retired and she assumed were having a short break in the area as advised by the marketing effort for the town. They had smiled and said "hello" politely as she entered but, having little conversation left for each other, had thereafter both stared at her from time to time, trying perhaps to work out why she was here alone and why she seemed rather upset. The couple on her right were considerably younger and clearly very much in love. They even held hands at one point while the husband buttered his toast awkwardly with his other hand before they both giggled. She wore both an engagement ring and a wedding ring and he wore a matching though chunkier version of the wedding ring. Were they newly-weds, Helen wondered? Perhaps they were young parents who had managed to escape from their children for a rare and brief opportunity to enjoy the love which had brought them together in the first place. Whatever their story Helen envied them and appreciated the fact that they had no time to wonder about her or anyone else around them for that matter.

Marie appeared from the kitchen and asked Helen if she would like more coffee or toast. There was plenty of both on the table in front of her and Helen wondered if she was really making sure that she was okay and that whichever bastard of a man who had stood her up the night before had not done any permanent damage.

"I'm fine, thank you," Helen replied sharply, covering all possible reasons for the inquiry.

Helen ate every last morsel of food on the plate and five of the six half slices of toast, washed down with all of the coffee from the cafetiere. She knew she might regret the quantity of liquid she had consumed later on her journey home but for now she was filling up and getting her money's worth.

She made it to her room without encountering her hostess, much to her relief, applied the minimum of essential make-up and finished packing. Then with a deep breath she gathered both her luggage and her resolve and headed downstairs to pay and make good her escape.

Marie was waiting at the foot of the stairs as if she was either worried Helen would do a runner or was concerned about her well being.

"Everything okay?" she asked.

"Yes, thank you," Helen replied pointedly, not keen to have any more unsolicited sympathy. "The room was very comfortable, thank you, and breakfast was lovely."

"I hope you weren't too disappointed after last night," Marie added, fishing for some background details.

"Everything went fine last night, thank you very much," Helen found herself saying in something of a huff. "Now if you don't mind I need to get back home to my husband and children."

"Of course, dear. That's probably for the best all round," said Marie and again she patted Helen's shoulder reassuringly.

Helen left the house at speed and her wheel spin threw up some gravel as she sped out of the driveway and headed home. What had that awful woman meant," probably for the best"? Of course it was for the best. Helen had a brave caring husband and had doubted him unfairly. What did that bitch Marie know about it? Had she thought Helen was slipping out to meet somebody else? She had a good mind to go back and tell her a thing or two, but as usual did not. Instead she kept driving home, rationalising things in her head as best she could.

What damage had actually been done? As long as Jimmy hadn't seen her at the caravan site, and she was almost certain he had not, then probably none. As long as she could get back home before her children got back from their Granny and Grandpa's house and before Jimmy got home from tidying up the paperwork following the arrest of that thug, then nobody would be any the wiser as to her foolishness. There was a chance that he had already headed home after the arrest and was back at an otherwise empty family home, but on the basis that she had received no phone call, it seemed unlikely. She drove with purpose, determined never to doubt her husband again. If her guilty trip to Girvan went unnoticed she resolved to make things up to Jimmy, even if he didn't realise that she felt such a need. She would get his favourite meal ready; a simple down to earth mince and potatoes with some of his favourite beers from the local brewery. The children would be shattered after being spoiled by her mother and step-father, so she would pack them off to bed early and then attempt a romantic evening, the likes of which they hadn't enjoyed for years.

She felt she owed Jimmy something special and remembered that although it had never been repeated, Jimmy had once come off night shift and handcuffed her to the bed while still wearing his uniform. They had made very energetic love together before Jimmy finally released her, showered and went to sleep. She knew they had both enjoyed it at the time but the moment had never reoccurred and after the children came along they had always seemed too tired to be as adventurous again. Tonight would be different if she could just get back in time. She would wear her sexiest underwear and a skirt far shorter than she would ever wear outside. Then she would make love to Jimmy in a way she was now sure he hadn't experienced for years. He could handcuff her to the bed or anything else he wanted to do just as long as he forgave her without ever finding out that she had doubted him. She just had to get home before he realised what she had done, where she had been, and what she had seen.

"Get out the fucking way," she screamed at an elderly gentleman wearing a cap who was driving a brand new Ford at a maximum speed of 30 miles an hour, despite the speed limit being 60, the roads being otherwise clear and driving conditions perfect.

Chapter Forty Four - Jimmy Returns Home to a Surprise

Jimmy awoke in the caravan at the unusually late time of half past nine and initially wondered where he was. Slowly but surely the smell of fresh coffee and frying bacon in a confined space reminded him that he was not at home and he was not with his wife Helen. He was still sleepy but realised he had to return to reality that day whether he liked it or not. That meant the uncomfortable issue of going home and pretending to his wife that he had been away on a relaxing fishing weekend with old Police College friends rather than enjoying a few days of infidelity with a victim of crime who was now his mistress, if that was still the term. Bit on the side, maybe. Whatever the modern term for it, he had been unfaithful to his wife and guilt was setting in as he looked ahead to returning to the family home they shared with their children. He got up slowly and showered, returning naked to the galley area of the caravan and grabbing Marion round the waist.

"I need to go home today. You understand that?"

"I know," said Marion in a matter of fact way which he found reassuring. "It was nice to spend a weekend together without having to rush everything, and it isn't finished yet. You get that bacon butty inside you while I shower and we will see what happens after that. You don't need to be home too early do you?"

Jimmy sat down at the table with a mug of fresh filtered coffee and a bacon roll overflowing with tomato ketchup. As he ate he looked back towards the kitchen area as Marion let her dressing gown slip to the floor and walked slowly to the shower. There wasn't any real rush after all, he decided.

By the time Jimmy Bell drove off from the caravan site in the afternoon after yet another shower, he was shattered. The nature of his job was such that he was used to long hours but this was a deep down exhausted feeling. Sheer sexual exhaustion at that. Fortunately for him, the coffee and the relatively early hour meant that he wasn't actually sleepy; just dog tired. He figured as soon as he got home he would be able to head off to bed fairly early. There was little chance of his wife wanting to do anything but talk about her mother and step-father, and he knew she would let him slope off after a few minutes of grisly details if he listened dutifully with a concerned expression on his face. An early night before returning to the office sounded ideal. All he had to do was stay awake on the journey home.

Jimmy found himself struggling to keep his eyes open after about 40 minutes on the road. The first stretch had been winding country roads but as soon as he got on the main motorway to Glasgow he rarely had to turn the wheel or change gear and fatigue started to kick in. After opening his window and singing along to the radio for 10 minutes or so he realised that he was going to be a danger to other road users and pulled off the motorway and to look for a cafe. After a tour of the outskirts of South Glasgow he found a place with a busy car park and parked up, relieved to be able to rest his eyes.

His plan had been to close his eyes for a few minutes and then have a coffee and a brisk walk before continuing but sleep overtook him now and he dosed for half an hour. He was awoken by a loud knock on the car window and lowered it to see a member of staff, possibly the owner, standing close to the glass.

"Yes?" Jimmy asked, still groggy from sleep.

"Are you okay?" asked the middle aged lady in black with an immaculately clean apron over her skirt.

"Yes, thanks," replied Jimmy rather annoyed at being disturbed.

"Then perhaps you would like to either use my cafe or move on. This isn't a truck stop and other customers have been unable to park since you arrived."

Jimmy was about to tell the woman what she could do with her cafe but stopped himself, aware that if she complained to the local police for any reason it could get embarrassing for him.

"Sorry about that," he said. "I must have dozed off for a minute or two. Time for a coffee."

He smiled and the owner of the cafe forced a smile in return. A coffee was hardly going to make up for a few car loads of lost customers but at least she had made her point to the sleeping occupant of the car taking up a space in her car park.

Jimmy still felt groggy and knew a coffee would him wake him up before the rest of the drive home. He was annoyed at being disturbed and would have driven somewhere else just to spite the cafe owner but he didn't know the area and he might have ended up driving around for a while to find somewhere else with little success. As he entered the cafe the smell of home baking hit his nostrils and he decided a coffee and perhaps a slice of that delicious looking carrot cake might be in order.

After a second cup of coffee, a slice of black forest gateau and a reconciliatory chat , Jimmy resumed his journey home, still tired but feeling refreshed enough to be safe. It was late on in the afternoon now and he was likely to arrive just in time for tea, a meal which he no longer really needed thanks to Angela's home baking. He had texted Helen and received a pleasant reply which suggested all was well on the home front. With a bit of luck she would have prepared a light meal and he could slip off for an early night afterwards. God knows he needed sleep badly now.

Chapter Forty Five - George Milne must Die

Alone and still dazed from his recent beating, Stevie Spider Webb sat in his secure room at the State Mental Hospital going over in his mind the events of his recent few days of freedom, and the frustrated attempt to kill George Milne and his girlfriend Janine McGovern.

A voice in his head which sounded suspiciously like Milne's kept repeating, "Well, that could have gone better."

He had been within feet of being able to kill Janine and Milne would have been next if it hadn't been for the intervention of his mystery attacker.

"Who the fuck was that?" he asked himself. Whoever it was he had been on hand and sufficiently proficient in the art of violence to stop Spider; no mean feat in his own modest opinion.

The only logical explanation he could think of was that Milne had employed a minder as soon as he heard that Spider was free. That was strange, as the police would undoubtedly have offered some form of protection to the couple. If Milne had turned that down and gone private, he must have had a reason. The fact that the bodyguard had legged it before the police arrived suggested to him that the minder, and by implication Milne, had something to hide. Whatever it was it must be something pretty dodgy. His mind turned back to events surrounding his initial arrest as he tried to piece together exactly how George Milne had become involved. He couldn't put his finger on it but given time, and he had plenty of time on his hands, he would figure it out.

Spider had been thoroughly checked over at the hospital under the watchful eyes of three of the largest policemen he had ever seen. Despite suffering concussion, four broken ribs, a broken wrist and massive bruising to his entire body he had still attempted to break free from his guards. It had been a futile gesture of defiance which the police officers had enjoyed subduing; their orders seemed to be clear: keep Webb in custody at all costs and no questions would be asked regarding restraint techniques. After all, any further injuries and bruises would go unnoticed. As a result of his further violent outbreak Spider found himself not only heavily drugged with painkillers amongst other medications but also securely bound within a straight-jacket. As per standard procedures his restraints were checked regularly in theory to protect his health and safety in keeping with his human rights. In practice though it was all about ensuring the health, safety and human rights of those whose job it was to keep him locked up.

Spider gave up trying to make sense of recent events in his life and instead returned to his favourite theme; after all, everyone needs a hobby. He began rocking back and forward on his cot, chanting quietly to himself like a demented monk. The chant had nothing to do with Zen Buddhism though. Had anyone chosen to listen in they would have heard him repeat over and over again, "George Milne must die, George Milne must die."

Chapter Forty Six - Hail the Conquering Hero

Jimmy pulled into his driveway with an audible sigh of relief. He had felt himself almost nod off twice in the last stretch of the journey. On one of the occasions he had even swerved and only just managed to stay on the road.

"I need to sleep, sleep, sleep," he kept saying to himself.

His wife's car was in the driveway parked to one side for a change, allowing him easy access to his preferred parking spot. That was odd, he thought to himself as he got out of his car. He was certain his wife Helen deliberately parked there most days simply to annoy him.

"Sleep, sleep," a voice in his head kept repeating.

He walked into the house ready for a barrage of questions about the fishing trip but was surprised when his wife appeared from the kitchen and simply gave him a long and passionate kiss on the lips. He knew his breath must be foul from the journey, coffee and cakes but Helen seemed unaffected. For her part she tasted rather nice and smelled even better. His detective skills identified her favourite perfume which she reserved for special occasions and as she headed back towards the kitchen he became aware of the unmistakable smell of mince and tatties cooking there. This was his favourite meal and he would have been looking forward to it if he wasn't still full from the earlier cakes and dog tired after the weekend's exertions. He also noticed that Helen was wearing a rather short skirt under an apron and a low cut blouse which was also of a sheer material. In a moment of panic he wondered if he had forgotten their wedding anniversary again but he quickly calculated that he had several months to prepare for that. What on earth was going on?

He shouted through to the kitchen that he was going to shower and change and headed upstairs praying that he would manage a decent plateful of food to avoid upsetting his wife and also that he would still be able to get to bed early and sleep. As he reached the half landing he suddenly noticed the dog which didn't bark; or more accurately he became aware of the lack of squabbling children in the house. Descending to the door of the kitchen he asked his wife;

"Where are the children?"

"Mum offered to keep them over till tomorrow," replied Helen, omitting the fact that they had spent the previous night there without her. "I thought we could have a romantic evening together, just me and you. The way it used to be."

Helen walked slowly over to Jimmy and placed one hand behind his head and the other firmly on his crotch which was still rather raw from recent overuse.

"You have a relaxing shower while I finish dinner," Helen whispered in his ear. "Your dressing gown is on the bed. No need to get dressed again. Hardly worth it really. I've bought a few of your favourite beers to go with dinner too or would you prefer a glass of wine?"

Jimmy forced a smile, ignoring the discomfort in the front of his trousers.

"A glass of wine please. I'll just pop up and shower. You smell nice. I should have known something was up."

Jimmy headed back upstairs for a shower, planning to take a dangerous level of painkillers and to rub enough cream on his privates to ease the impending further abrasion. There was a tube of a cream they used for bee stings which contained an anaesthetic as well as an antiseptic and he wondered if Helen would notice if he used it all. He felt guilty it was true. If only his wife was always as sexy and romantically inclined as this, although he could hardly blame her in any way for his recent infidelity. That was entirely his fault. He just wished that women throwing themselves at him weren't like buses; you waited ages for one...

Chapter Forty Seven - George at Home

George and Janine returned home to Coatshill after being interviewed by the police in Ayrshire, two days after Spider's re-arrest. The interviews had been mercifully short, due to Spider's expected full recovery and the fact that he could be prosecuted for whatever it transpired he had done while on the loose at a leisurely pace, now that he was back in the safety of secure custody. They entered the house and looked round. Somebody had been in the house and gone through their possessions. Janine screamed and ran to the bedroom to check her jewellery which she was surprised to find was still in the usual drawer where she had left it. A good look round established that nothing appeared to be missing. Things had been moved, evidenced by the location of objects and dust marks but they could find nothing actually missing. Even the twenty pound note left out to pay the milkman was still sitting near the back door.

Janine was keen to phone the police but George was reluctant. His initial relief at finding their possessions still there had turned to a growing sense of unease. If whoever had broken in, without breaking anything in the process, had left the jewellery and the loose cash lying about then it stood to reason they were looking for something else; something specific. George stood at the kitchen sink and looked at his shed. He needed to check the floorboards but didn't want to arouse Janine's suspicion.

"I need to think about this before we phone the police. After all, whoever it was hasn't stolen anything. What do we report? A lack of the theft of our things? I'm going to my shed to think it over."

"Can you not just stay here and think? For Christ's sake why do men need a bloody shed to think in? Okay on you go, I'm having a cup of tea. I'll make you one once you've got that old turnip of a brain in order again."

George could tell Janine was angry but knew it was at the invasion of their privacy, and not at him. If he had been at fault there would have been no offer of a cup of tea when he returned. Of course she wasn't angry at him. He had saved their lives only a few days before. That had to count for something, even with his luck.

He walked slowly towards the shed, trying to look like somebody deep in thought rather than a man panicking that his stash of stolen money might have been stolen again. He was so focused on the task in hand that he failed to see Bob Brown behind the lace curtain of his window, phone in hand ready to report any further illegal spread of weed killer or plant thefts. He had heard George's car park outside and immediately returned to his usual practice of observing everything his neighbour did, oblivious of having missed a real break in some days before.

George's pace gathered speed as he got closer to the shed and he rushed inside. The tools appeared to have been moved slightly but the area around the floor panel appeared to be undisturbed. He looked round unnecessarily to make sure nobody had followed him and moved the crate of beer making apparatus. Underneath, the dirt was untouched. He was about to put it back in place when panic set in and he lifted the board to check the package of money was still in its rightful place. To his immense relief it was there just as he had left it. He slipped a bundle of a thousand pounds' worth of twenties into his pocket and carefully replaced everything as it had been.

He waited in the draughty shed long enough for Janine to believe he had been deep in thought. She could call the police if she really wanted. They were unlikely to be overly interested in a phantom robbery where nothing had been taken. The more he thought about it the more he was certain the break-in had been an attempt by Spider to find them, and the police would surely agree.

He put this thought to Janine when he went back inside, and she shivered, thinking of what might have happened if they had been at the house when Spider had broken in. Mind you, she thought, as long as George was there she would be safe. He had floored Spider twice and now appeared to have it down to a fine art.

She made him the promised mug of tea and brought it through to the front room where she found him sitting in his favourite chair watching the news. She placed the steaming drink on the table beside him with three chocolate digestives - he had to keep his strength up - and gave him a long, passionate kiss on the lips, which blocked his view of the weather forecast for three whole minutes.

"What was that for?" he asked bemused, whilst wondering whether or not it would rain the following day.

"You're a strange one, George Milne, that's for sure. But you're my hero. Don't be too late getting to bed and I'll prove it."

With that she walked out of the room moving her shapely figure from side to side in a very suggestive manner. George watched her go realising he wouldn't get a chance to read his book that night. Life was strange, he thought, rather than himself. He found women possibly stranger. It didn't matter much though. He and Janine were both safe now. Spider was in secure custody and George still had the money to make sure he never had to work again. Whoever had beaten up Spider had done them both a favour. Judging by Janine's manner towards him ever since, and tonight in particular, they had done George a bigger favour still. He wouldn't have been surprised if Inspector Bell had done it himself and then done a quick lap of the block to avoid any blame. Perhaps he would never know who his mystery saviour had been.

He put the empty mug down on his side table and switched off the television. Time for bed, he decided, and whatever Janine had in store for him. After all, he could catch the weather forecast on the early news programme in the morning.

Body and Soul

Two very different men are on a pathway to a meeting which will change both their lives forever. One is a Scottish ex-soldier, ex-boxer, ex-husband, ex-father and ex-drunk struggling to turn his life around. The other, the CEO of an American multi-national, has both wealth and power. They do not know each other and only the American believes he knows the true purpose of their meeting. In fact both have been duped in different ways and as their lives begin to unravel they must try to deal with the truth if they can. Only one has the skills and determination to survive.

After failing to wake Frank he dragged him into the shower which conveniently only produced cold water and turned it on full. The effect wasn't immediate, but slowly the old fighting, kicking Frank began to re-appear, curse the first house guest he had had for six months and try to throw him out. After an initial but futile attempt to punch Paddy's lights out Frank calmed down enough to recognise his visitor.

Made in the USA
Columbia, SC
25 July 2017